THE KINGFISHER BOOK OF

HORSE & PONY STORIES

With special thanks to Margaret Manby, expert in all things equine — J.O.

KINGFISHER
a Houghton Mifflin Company imprint
222 Berkeley Street
Boston, Massachusetts 02116
www.houghtonmifflinbooks.com

First published in 2005
2 4 6 8 10 9 7 5 3 1

LIBRARY OF CONGRESS CATALOGING–IN–PUBLICATION DATA
has been applied for.

ISBN 0-7534-5850-0
ISBN 978-07534-5850-1

Printed in China
ITR/0605/SNPLFG/CLSN(CLSN)/140MA/C

THE KINGFISHER BOOK OF
HORSE &
PONY
STORIES

COMPILED BY JENNY OLDFIELD

KINGFISHER

BOSTON

Contents

Introduction

What is it that we love about horses and ponies? Some people say that it's the intelligence shining in those big, dark eyes or the beauty of that arched neck, broad back, and slender legs. For others, it's the sheer speed of the creature, sprinting free across green fields or throwing up a cloud of dust on a scorched desert trail. Whatever it is, once you get to know horses, it's easy to get hooked!

When you get up close, a horse is so big that it can be scary. It towers over you, its hooves are hard, its kick fast and fierce. And when you climb onto its back, there are stirrups and a saddle to help you—but no handlebars or steering wheel! Oh, and when it moves and you're sitting up high, there's a sway that you don't expect, a lively step, and a move from walk to trot, from trot to canter and then gallop. Will it stop if you use the reins? Will it swerve at the fence, or will it jump clean over it? Whoa!

So it's a big challenge when you ride a horse or pony for the first time—as well as a dream come true. But why does this magnificent creature do us the huge favor of carrying us safely from point A to point B? Why not just throw us off and break free? I'm grateful for it, of course, but it's always a mystery. So is the way its brain is wired to flee from invisible danger and to spook at the littlest thing. You have to be ready to think fast and to pick yourself up when you fall off. Get right back in the saddle and try again. That is, if you're lucky enough to be able to ride. I wasn't, until a few years back, when I began to write stories about animals. I learned all there is to know about cats and dogs, hamsters and hedgehogs—and ponies! Then I decided that if I was going to *really* write about horses, I had to get up there and ride them. So I put my first foot in a stirrup, swung into the saddle . . . and the love affair began. Me and the riding school pony in the indoor arena. Me and a good friend's Connemara-thoroughbred cross, riding down country roads. Me and my own purebred gray Arabian, Merlin, galloping through the woods . . .

I hope, when you read the stories in this collection—all of them are original, and all are written by people who love their subject—you can sense the wonder of the horse. Travel back in time to ancient Greece and Japan and across continents to Canada, North America, and Europe. See how the horse plays its part in these fantastic stories. If you long for your own pony, you can read here about kids like you, whose dreams sometimes do come true. And always, throughout the book, you'll notice the admiration that we writers have for the horses and ponies that feature here—perhaps even more than admiration. For me, it's a mixture of love and awe.

When readers ask me (and they often do), "Of all the animals you write about, which are your favorites?," I never hold back. "Horses and ponies," I tell them. And that's the truth. Horses and ponies. They always will be.

Jenny Oldfield

The Last Roundup

JENNY OLDFIELD

His old bones ached.
Three days in the saddle herding cattle really got to you when you'd notched up 50-plus years on this hard, dry, dusty earth. Sixty, actually, though Sam Gibb didn't admit that, even to himself.

"Yip! Yip!" The cowboys steered the cows wide of a stretch of willows, bunching them up the hillside to the right and then pressing them back into the gully bottom. One renegade cow broke away and had to be chased down from a ledge.

Oh boy, Captain! Sam let his sorrel quarter horse know how much he was looking forward to his bunk bed. By the end of the day, his job as the chief hand on the fall roundup for the Cross Seven Ranch would be done.

"Yip!" Bobbie Austin drove the renegade back into the heaving bunch of brown-and-white Herefords. Dressed in leather chaps, a plaid shirt, and a dirt-encrusted Stetson, she didn't look like a blonde, blue-eyed 13 year old—more like one of the old hands.

"Glad you brought the kid along, huh?" her father grinned. Warren Austin was the boss of the Cross Seven.

"Hmm," Sam grunted.

"Hey, c'mon—Bobbie rides that Appaloosa like she was born in the saddle!"

"Hmm," Sam said again. Compliments weren't his line. In fact, wild horses wouldn't drag one out of him. He hadn't wanted the boss' kid tagging along in the first place.

"Bringing a herd of Herefords down from the mountains before winter sets in ain't no job for a schoolkid," he'd objected to his boss.

"I know, Sam," Warren admitted. "But if Bobbie says she wants to do something, ain't nothing gonna shift the idea out of that skull until it's done."

Sam grumbled, but when the boss said "jump," you jumped. He'd warned Bobbie that no way would she get special treatment. "You sleep on a hard bedroll under the stars like the rest of us," he'd rasped at her. "You track steers and rope 'em in until your hands are blistered red raw and you're almost dead in the saddle, and then you take the night watch—get it?"

Frowning, Bobbie listened to her orders. She'd looked Sam directly in his lined, unshaven face. "Sure!" she'd said.

Now Sam reined Captain back and watched Warren ride up alongside his daughter. *Say one thing for the kid,* he thought, noting the way that she drove the runaway cow into line and then reined back to talk to her pa, *she sure rides that Appaloosa like a real cowboy!*

"Easy, girl!" Bobbie settled La Gata into a smooth trot. She tilted back her hat and quickly wiped her sticky forehead. One more day of hard riding, and they were through!

The Appaloosa jostled her dad's sturdy bay horse. The tack jingled, and their hooves ground the dirt underfoot in a steady, thudding rhythm.

"So what d'you think of herding cows?" Warren teased. "Kinda boring, ain't it?"

"No, Dad, it's been cool!" Bobbie protested. Thrilling, even. When you cornered a cow on a rocky ledge no more than two feet wide, with a 30-foot drop into a dry gully, and you eyeballed that bellowing critter and brought her safely down, no way did Bobbie call that boring.

Okay, so she had grit in her hair, her ears, and every seam of her shirt and jeans. She didn't smell good, and she wouldn't want to meet the guys from school before she'd had an hour-long shower. But the cattle drive had been a real blast.

And her beloved, graceful, beautiful La Gata—The Cat—well, she'd been fantastic! Fast when she needed to be, sure-footed on the rocks, alert to every movement and sound on the pine-covered mountainside.

"Good for you, Bobbie!" Warren grinned.

Bobbie grinned back. "Good for La Gata!" she replied.

They were bringing the herd along a ridge, around five hours from home, when it happened.

To the west were the high peaks of the southern Rockies— dark blue shadows in the far distance. To the east, the land dropped away in a wide stretch of scrubland that merged into endless prairie. The herd was strung out two or three deep along the ridge, calves trotting alongside their mothers, the older cows sensing that the ranch was almost within sight.

Surveying the scene from the rear, Sam saw that his half-dozen riders were stretched to the limit. Like the cows, they were strung out, with gaps of maybe 160 feet between them. This left too much room for a steer to cut loose. Once that happened, others might follow, and all heck would break loose.

So he and Captain were already on tenterhooks, noting an edginess in the herd—too much jostling and barging on the narrow trail—when the rustlers struck.

There were ten riders swooping down the hillside, cutting the herd in half. They rode through the cattle at a gallop and then reined their horses around and began pushing the front section back up the hill toward another dirt track. Warren Austin was at the front, along with a guy named Bill Sallee, but the two of them couldn't stop the scattering of the panicking herd.

"Darn!" Sam muttered, spitting out a gob of phlegm. He dug his spurs into Captain's side. He'd leave what was left of the herd in the care of the ranch boss and the others and cut up across the hillside to meet the rustlers on the top track. With luck, Sam could cut them off before they reached their hidden cattle trucks.

Bobbie saw Sam go, understood his aim, and in a split second decided to follow. "Go, La Gata!" she whispered.

Her Appaloosa raced after Captain. She swallowed the ground, streaking uphill with her ears back and her head straining forward, white mane flying, hooves tearing up the tumbleweed and thornbushes.

By the time Sam reached the top track, he felt the kid by his side. They charged along the flat, desperate to cut off a bunch of five riders and around 50 of the Herefords. Ahead of them, a giant cattle truck waited in a wide, flat clearing.

"Yee-haw!" Sam yelled, taking off his hat and waving it above his head.

The cry startled the cattle. Their heads went down, and the lead cow lunged off the track, back down the hillside, taking around 20 others with her.

Still at full gallop, Bobbie saw the rustlers rein back their horses and watch their quarry disappear. Their leader signaled for the gang to retreat. The truck driver, seeing that the game was up, started his engine and began to trundle down the dirt track. The rustlers regrouped, bunching together to listen to orders before racing off up the mountain.

"Cool!" Bobbie thought. Her heart was pounding, La Gata's flanks were heaving, but they'd shown those rustlers a thing or two!

She pressed on behind Sam and Captain, both horses going at a steady canter toward the truck.

"I've got your number!" Sam shouted, warning the truck owner that he could expect a visit from the sheriff.

But the sound of the engine drowned out his voice. The driver stepped on the accelerator. The monster machine gathered speed, bearing down on them.

"He's crazy!" Bobbie gasped. The track was narrow; there was nowhere for them to go.

"Back off!" Sam yelled, lurching sideways in the saddle as Captain reared up.

The truck kept on coming, the roar of its engine filling their ears.

La Gata spooked big-time. Up she went on her hind legs, fighting for her head, letting out a high whinny of fear.

There was the smell of diesel, the thunderous roll of huge wheels on dirt.

Sam struggled to bring Captain down and turn him to protect La Gata and Bobbie. "This guy ain't gonna stop!" he yelled at her.

The steel monster loomed over them.

Bobbie saw Captain swing around again and ditch his rider in the dirt, so Sam lay sprawled in the path of the truck. Then La Gata did something crazy. She reared up so high that she tipped backward, spilling Bobbie and landing off the track, legs pawing the air.

Bobbie thudded to the ground and rolled clear. She sensed Sam crawling out of the truck's way while Captain frantically scrambled up the steep hill. But poor La Gata was on her back, helpless, sliding down the mountain, crashing against trees and boulders.

Bobbie screamed. She shut her eyes. She opened them to a sharp, sudden explosion—the sound of a single gunshot.

"I had to do it," Sam said through gritted teeth. The gun was back in its holster, its deadly deed done.

La Gata lay still on the ground, her eyes closed.

Bobbie felt as though her heart had been torn out.

"Her front leg was busted," Sam explained. "There ain't no way the horse could've made it."

La Gata was dead. She lay against a pink granite rock. Her body was battered and bruised, her beautiful markings covered in dirt.

After the roar of the truck's engine, there was unbearable silence.

Bobbie's heartbreak turned to anger. She beat her fists against Sam's shoulders and chest.

Sam grunted with pain. He guessed that he'd busted a couple of ribs in the fall, but he didn't resist. Sure, the kid was mad at him. She'd ridden the Appaloosa ever since Warren Austin had first put her in the saddle.

"You didn't have to do that!" Bobbie cried. "You didn't have to shoot her!"

"She was hurting," Sam said. "She wasn't never gonna get up."

It was too much for Bobbie. For a second, she bent over, holding her aching stomach. Then she straightened up. "The trouble with you is that you've got no heart!" she told Sam. She made a lunge for the heavy gun hanging at his side.

The pain in his ribs slowed Sam down, but he was quick enough to stop her from taking the gun. He stared at her. "What did you wanna do—shoot me?"

She hated the way the old guy looked at her, his lips set in a hard line. More than that, she hated that La Gata was dead. She thought of the cruel guy in the truck and the men who swooped down the mountain to steal her dad's herd. In an instant, the whole world had turned bad.

So Bobbie ran.

Tears blinded her, staining her cheeks as she sprinted up the mountain, slipping, sliding, clinging onto tree roots, until she was out of sight, alone.

Out of breath, she looked up at patches of blue sky through

the branches of the tall pines, finding that she had run into a narrow gully with sheer rock on both sides. She slumped down onto the ground. Her hands trembled. Her whole body shook.

It was a while before Bobbie really took in her surroundings. She was high on the mountain now, almost at the snow line. The fall wind cut icy cold down the gully, whipping up the loose dirt.

And she wasn't as alone as she'd thought. The first sign was hoofprints, which the wind was rearranging. They pointed down to the dead end of the gully. Then there were sounds—perhaps a breath, a tiny movement. Or maybe Bobbie had imagined that. She began to look more closely.

A large creature stirred in a thicket of thornbushes. There was a glimpse of rich brown, the click of a hoof against rock.

"Captain?" Bobbie whispered. She edged forward.

Sam Gibb's horse had hidden deep in the gully. He had fled from the truck in a panic and taken shelter here. Bobbie crept toward him and saw that the big sorrel was still terrified.

"I know!" she whispered. "This is horrible. But you're okay now. Come on here to me, Captain. C'mon!"

The horse didn't stir. Every muscle was frozen, his eyes rolling in fear.

And when Bobbie glanced up to a ledge ten feet above him, she saw why.

Mountain lion! The big cat crouched, ready to pounce, front legs bent, head low against the rock, its bright eyes fixed on the horse. Its claws could tear the horse's tough hide; its jaws could rip through soft flesh.

Bobbie froze too. One false move could make the cat leap from the ledge.

The trapped horse didn't move a muscle. A loose rein swung in the wind.

Okay! Bobbie thought. She stooped to pick up a rock the size of her fist.

The yellow eyes glistened. The pupils were narrow slits. The cat crouched over the horse. It was Bobbie's job to find that target.

She threw the rock. It thudded against the hindquarters of the lion, who recoiled with a loud howl that echoed down the hillside. Way down the mountain, Warren Austin was helping Sam climb onto the back of his own horse. The men heard the howl and stopped what they were doing.

The mountain lion turned so fast that it was a blur of pale brown fur. Bobbie's aim had been good, and it triggered off a flight so swift that the cat was gone from the ledge before she even drew a breath.

Bobbie let out a long sigh. She would have killed that living, breathing, beautiful creature if she'd been able to. In a choice between horse and lion, the horse would always win.

She lowered her head. Then she took a few steps toward Captain. "Hey, boy!" she sighed.

Sam's horse answered with a soft snort and a shake of his head.

"Let's get out of here!" Bobbie said.

Later that day Sam Gibb took off his Stetson and turned the brim between his stubby, work-worn hands.

He stood with his boss outside the barn at Cross Seven Ranch.

"I owe you plenty," Warren Austin told him. The cows and calves were corralled and counted, ready to be trucked out to the lowland winter pasture. "What can I do to thank you?"

Sam shrugged. His gaze was fixed on the kid. She was doing chores around the barn, pouring feed into wooden mangers, letting the horses eat. He noted that she spent more time on Captain's feed than on the rest. "I reckon that's my last roundup," he mumbled. "These old ribs don't get fixed as fast as they used to."

The kid went about her jobs with the grim look that she'd worn since her Appaloosa had been shot.

Even when she'd ridden down the mountain on Captain and told Sam and her dad about the mountain lion, there'd been no gleam in her eyes. He'd thanked her for saving Captain, but she'd just shaken her head and walked away. But Sam noticed the time she was spending on grooming his horse and talking to Captain now that she thought no one was listening.

"You sure?" Warren checked with Sam. "If you leave, that's a big decision you've just made."

"I'm sure," Sam said. There was only so much punishment a man's body could take. From now on he would hang up his spurs and take it easy.

But there was one last thing he wanted to do before he left.

Sam walked stiffly across the corral.

Bobbie heard him approach. She still couldn't look him in the eye without feeling her heart lurch and seeing La Gata lying against the pink granite rock.

"Hey," Sam grunted.

Bobbie ignored him.

"Captain owes you his life," Sam said. "And I reckon he knows it."

Bobbie's hand went up around the sorrel's neck.

"He's a good horse," Sam said. "Loyal, a hard worker, the type of horse that stays with you to the end."

"The best," Bobbie acknowledged.

Captain nuzzled her hand with his soft nose.

This was harder than Sam had figured—saying these next few words. "I quit my job, so he's yours," he muttered.

Bobbie frowned. "Mine?"

"Yeah. You saved him, so now you can have him." Captain should belong to the kid. That was the right thing to do.

Warren Austin stood, arms folded, watching his daughter talk to the old cowboy. He saw her raise her head at last, and there were no frown lines creasing her face. In that instant, his

daughter had stopped hating the world she lived in.

"Hey, Captain!" Bobbie breathed. She put both arms around the sorrel's neck. "You and I are a team!"

Old Sam Gibb nodded and then stepped quietly back into the deep shadow of the barn.

The Rivals

GILL HARVEY

There was a hush as the huge white doors of the Winter Riding School swung open. The audience had already seen the power and grace of the white Lipizzan stallions as they danced and pirouetted beneath the sparkling chandeliers. They had seen the trust and commitment that fused each horse and rider together. Now they were going to see something special.

Three riders rode into the hall on gleaming Lipizzans. The gilded bridles and scarlet saddlecloths of the earlier performances were gone; these horses wore only black bridles and plain green saddlecloths under saddles without stirrups. They came to a halt. The riders, solemn and elegant, took off their black two-cornered hats and bowed to the portrait of Emperor Karl VI that hung under the arch at the end of the hall.

Klaus held his breath. He had been a student at the Spanish Riding School for more than two years, but the spectacle of the "airs above the ground" still filled him with awe. He concentrated on Chief Rider Wolfgang, who was riding Maestoso Bonavista, the best *caprioleur* of all of the school stallions. As the horse soared into the air and kicked out his hind legs in a perfect capriole, Klaus felt a nudge. It was his schoolmate, Hans.

"That will be me one day," whispered Hans. His eyes glittered.

"Out there, performing a capriole."

Klaus said nothing. He looked away, his eyes returning to Wolfgang, who seemed glued to Maestoso's back despite the lack of stirrups. Klaus usually ignored Hans when he began to boast.

Hans leaned close to Klaus' ear. "I wonder where you'll be then?" he asked softly.

Klaus whipped around and glared at Hans angrily. It was exactly the reaction Hans wanted. His eyes lit up with glee. Klaus opened his mouth to snap at his rival and then changed his mind. Hans really wasn't worth it.

But later that night Klaus lay awake, unable to shake off his anger. He knew exactly where he wanted to be in the future. Like Hans, he wanted to be right here in Vienna at the Spanish Riding School. He longed to become a chief rider too. It filled him with cold, helpless fury when Hans implied that he wouldn't make it— but there was only one way to achieve his goal. He had to work hard, listen to everything he was taught, and learn from his mistakes. Above all, he had to understand each horse he rode as though the horse was his best friend.

Hans had been confident of success right from the start. His family was one of the wealthiest in Vienna, and he had learned to ride before he could walk. Klaus had grown up in the countryside, in the hills near the Piber stud farm, where the Lipizzans were bred. He had spent hours watching the foals frolic in the fields, but although he loved horses, he could barely ride when he was taken on as a student. The trainers said it didn't matter—Wolfgang himself had told him so. One day, not long after joining the school, Klaus had been stiff and sore from many hours of riding, and his face must have shown his despair.

"It is easier to teach someone the right way from the start than to correct their mistakes," the chief rider had said.

Klaus remembered those words every time Hans gloated over him. The two teenagers seemed destined to be rivals. Few students

passed on to the next stage in a rider's training, and the chances
of them both succeeding were slim. Time had passed. Other riders
had come and gone. Klaus knew that the chief riders must come to
a decision soon, but he had no idea when.

∾∾

Klaus slept at last but woke with the dawn. He made his way to
the stables to begin the day's work. Inside, light slanted down
upon the shining white rumps of the Lipizzan horses, all quietly
dozing or chewing on mouthfuls of hay. The smell was
comfortingly familiar—warm, earthy horse, rich saddle leather, and
tangy brass polish mingled with the fine dust of fresh straw.

Klaus walked along the line of stalls. Each had an elegant black
post outside with a brass-framed nameplate at the top, but Klaus
didn't need to read them. He knew them all by heart.

He stopped at a stall labeled "Favory Borina." The horse inside
whinnied.

"Hello, Favory," murmured Klaus with a smile. It always

cheered him to hear the stallion's greeting, and he scratched the horse's neck for a few moments before starting work. This horse had taught him to ride in the time-honored tradition: the older school horses taught the student riders, while the older riders taught the young stallions. Favory would never respond to poor riding, so Klaus developed a good, strong position in the saddle.

The morning chores were half done when Klaus heard Florian, one of the chief riders, calling along the line of stalls.

"Klaus! Hans!"

Klaus stuck his head out of Favory's stall and called, "Here!" Hans did the same, farther down.

Florian beckoned them over. "Hans, Wolfgang wants you to ride Maestoso Bonavista in the hall after the morning exercise. Klaus, Christian is sick. Pluto Ancona needs practice for the performance on Sunday, so tomorrow you are to take Christian's place in the morning exercise."

Klaus stared at Florian, his mouth dropping open. Hans' face had split into a triumphant grin. "Maestoso Bonavista!" he crowed. "What d'you think of that, Klaus?"

Klaus was still struggling to take in the news. This was surely some kind of test. Riding the wonderful *caprioleur* was an enormous honor—but preparation for a performance was a greater responsibility, especially since spectators were allowed in.

"I think I prefer my own task," he said quietly.

He returned to Favory's stall to think it over. Pluto Ancona was a talented young stallion but shy and nervous—a little like Klaus himself. Riding him in front of the public would mean keeping him calm and focused, so Klaus would have to be calm too. Maestoso Bonavista, on the other hand, was a spirited horse with great strength and intelligence. He had been known to humiliate riders who thought too much of themselves. Klaus smiled wryly. He could see that neither rider would find his task easy.

The news soon spread. All of the grooms and students chattered excitedly at the idea of Hans riding Maestoso. Many of them crowded into the galleries of the hall to watch the spectacle— and Klaus could not resist going too.

They fell silent as the chief riders entered the hall on foot. Next, Wolfgang's groom walked in, leading Maestoso. Hans, dressed in his gray student's uniform, came last. He took off his hat and bowed low before the portrait of Karl VI. Then, on a signal from Wolfgang, he mounted and took up the reins.

As Hans rode the majestic stallion around the hall, Klaus watched him closely, noting his schoolmate's faults. Hans had a tendency to be heavy-handed and pull on the reins, a habit developed by riding headstrong ponies from an early age. The trainers had worked tirelessly to cure him of it, but they had still not succeeded completely. Klaus could see that Hans had fallen into his old habit. It wasn't surprising—after all, he was bound to fear losing control. But Maestoso wouldn't normally put up with riding like that.

Things seemed to be going well. Wolfgang asked Hans to walk, trot, and canter around the hall in circles and figure eights, collecting the stallion's stride and then extending it again. These were the basics that the students had learned in the last two years, and Hans looked at ease in the saddle. Then, to the spectators' surprise, Wolfgang called Hans over and instructed him to ask for *passage*— the first move of the *haute école*, or high school of equitation.

The students held their breath. *Passage* was the high-stepping, slow-motion trot in which the horse seemed almost to float above the ground. Everyone knew how to ask for it in theory—but would Hans be able to handle it on a horse like Maestoso?

Hans rode the horse away, down to the bottom of the hall. Then he turned and gave the aids for *passage*. Like a dream, Maestoso did as he was asked in a beautiful straight line down the middle of the hall.

In spite of himself, Klaus was impressed. The stallion was perhaps overbending his head a little, no doubt from Hans' pressure on the reins, but other than that, it could have been Wolfgang himself in the saddle. Right in front of the chief riders, Maestoso came to a halt. Spontaneously, the little group of grooms and students broke into applause, and Hans gave a smug smile.

Hans was unprepared for what happened next. Maestoso wanted his say. Without warning, he leaped into the air and, at the top of the leap, kicked out his hind legs in a spectacular capriole. Hans didn't stand a chance. He flew over the horse's head and landed at Wolfgang's feet in an undignified heap.

The applause turned into snickers, silenced only by a stern glance from Wolfgang. As Klaus watched Hans get to his feet, red-faced and flustered, he felt his mouth become dry. The chief riders had chosen carefully when they decided on the tests.

"We want you to stick to the basics," said Wolfgang. "No *haute école*. Just the essentials of good dressage, performed well."

Klaus listened intently. At least it is not the performance itself, he kept telling himself. In the morning exercise he could ride his own routine, concentrating on maintaining his bond with the horse.

He had spent most of the afternoon before in Pluto's stall, grooming the stallion and getting to know him. The stables had been full of laughter about Hans' misfortune, but Klaus did not join in or even allow himself to feel pleased. He would have to ride exceptionally well himself in order to keep Pluto calm in the morning exercise.

And now the moment had arrived. Taking a deep breath, Klaus led Pluto from his stall and joined the other horses outside the riding hall. He heard the chatter of the spectators as they filled up the lofty white balconies. The noise died down as the music began and the huge white doors opened.

Klaus rode into the hall with the other horses and bowed to the portrait of Karl VI. Then he was on his own, riding Pluto beneath the gaze of the curious public. He must not, must not lose his concentration. Throughout the warm-up and the exercises that followed, he kept a constant, reassuring contact with the reins so that Pluto always knew he was there.

The other horses went on to practice the fluid movements of *haute école*—*passage*, then the rhythmic trotting on the spot that was called *piaffe*, stunning flying changes of leg while cantering across the hall, and tightly controlled pirouettes. But Klaus kept Pluto working at a simpler level and gradually felt the stallion relax.

As they neared the end of the session, Klaus began to settle down. He asked Pluto for a collected trot down the side of the hall and reveled in the graceful arch of the horse's neck as he responded.

They were halfway down when Klaus heard a howl—a child's cry of dismay that made the stallion tremble. Klaus' heart leaped into his mouth. He did not look up. He didn't need to, for fluttering into his path from the highest balcony was a child's bright purple umbrella.

Stay calm, he thought. *Don't panic.* With his legs firmly against the stallion's sides, he pushed him forward. *I am here*, he thought calmly, keeping his seat firm and his hands steady. *There is nothing to fear.*

The horrible umbrella rolled in front of Pluto, half open, as he stepped toward it. Klaus could sense the tension in the horse's body. Did the stallion trust him? He clamped his legs onto the horse's sides even more tightly. Pluto rolled his eyes and snorted. In three more strides he was there. One-two, one-two . . . neatly picking up his hooves, Pluto stepped over the umbrella and continued down the hall.

Klaus felt weak with relief. *Don't let it go now!* he scolded himself, as he began a final circuit of the hall. But outside, when he dismounted, the sound of applause faded in his ears, and his knees gave way beneath him.

That evening Hans and Klaus were each summoned before the chief riders. Klaus caught sight of Hans as he emerged from their room. His face was clouded with anger and disappointment. Klaus braced himself for his own meeting, but he was greeted with a smile.

"You are progressing well," Wolfgang said to him. "You show the most important skill of all, which is the ability to learn. Are you happy with us, Klaus?"

"Oh, yes, sir," said Klaus fervently.

"Then you may keep your place," Wolfgang told him. "You will be a student for a while yet, but you will surely advance, in time."

"Thank you, sir," stuttered Klaus.

He walked back to the stables feeling almost faint and went straight to Pluto Ancona's stall. The stallion greeted him with a whinny.

Klaus fished in his pocket for a sugar lump. "It's not much to give you, Pluto," he murmured as the horse licked the sugar from his fingers. "But maybe one day I'll be able to thank you properly."

A Horse Without Equal

ELIZABETH HOLLAND

Alexander crouched in the shadows, peering out at the bustling yard through a crack in the stall door. The stall was empty and had been for some time but smelled strongly of horses and the doves that roosted in the rafters. It was also very dusty. Alexander wrinkled his nose, hoping that he wouldn't sneeze. If Tyros, the head groom, caught him, he would be in serious trouble, even though he was the king of Macedonia's son.

He pressed his cheek against the door, trying to see more clearly. Outside in the yard, the head groom was in charge of stabling 50 or 60 new arrivals. It looked chaotic, but each horse had a place allotted to it. Tyros frowned and shouted instructions as the stable keepers guided the horses into their temporary homes, filling the manger with hay and the troughs with water. Many of the horses shuffled with their heads down, their coats dusty, and their eyes dull with fatigue. They had traveled long distances so that King Philip could have his pick of them.

Since he was old enough to ride, Alexander had yearned for the first sight of the traders coming across the plain. From the palace tower, he would watch the dust cloud resolve itself into groups of men and horses. There was no thrill like that of watching the proud horses flashing through the city's narrow

A HORSE WITHOUT EQUAL

streets, bearing the colors and flags of their breeders. Once they were safely stabled, however, that was it. The royal stables were not open to visitors, and Alexander knew it.

Now that he was 12, he had had enough. He deserved to see the horses that would be presented to his father. In his hiding place Alexander squared his shoulders. He wasn't afraid of Tyros.

The next moment, he almost leaped out of his skin as Tyros' rough voice said, "You'll have to put him in here. There's nowhere else."

The door rattled. Alexander flung himself to the back of the stable, panicking. The doves shot through a large gap in the corner of the roof, white wings flapping. It was the only way out. Alexander hoisted himself up onto the manger and clambered through the hole, just in time. He sat on the roof, afraid to move in case he made a sound, as the door swung open.

"You can't expect me to leave him here!" said a different voice. "This is a ruin! I wouldn't leave a donkey here, let alone the finest horse in generations!"

Tyros snorted. "It's all that's left. He'll be fine here."

The other man tried to argue with him, but Tyros interrupted. "Stable him here, or take him away. It's your choice, Popolos."

Curiosity gave Alexander the courage to sneak a look through the hole. Popolos was one of the best horsemen in Greece, breeder of the strongest and most beautiful horses in King Philip's stables. Alexander was a little disappointed to see a short, fat man with sweat patches on his tunic. As Alexander shrank back, Popolos led his horse into the stable, muttering under his breath. He filled the manger and groomed the horse himself, to Alexander's surprise. Most breeders allowed the palace grooms to take care of their charges. Without spotting the young boy peering through the gap in the roof, Popolos patted his horse and closed the stable door for the night. Alexander could relax. He stretched out his cramped

31

limbs and lowered himself carefully back down into the stall. Before leaving, he wanted to take a better look at the horse that Popolos had handled with such affection and pride.

Although the door was closed, light from the setting sun found a way through gaps in the door and walls. Alexander gazed openmouthed at the horse.

He was the most beautiful stallion Alexander had ever seen. Every line of his body was perfect, from the strong hindquarters and shoulders to the elegant head. The horse tossed his mane and snorted, one intelligent eye fixed on the boy. Alexander reached out tentatively and stroked his glossy black neck. The horse nudged him and blew warm air into his face. Alexander laughed in delight. "What a beauty you are!" he said, admiring the white star in the middle of his forehead. The horse nudged him again. Alexander could almost believe that he was agreeing with him. He longed to swing himself up onto the horse's back and ride as far and as fast as he could. This was the horse of his dreams.

"I'll see you tomorrow. I promise," he said, when he eventually tore himself away, clambering back up to the gap in the roof. He took one last look before sliding down to the ground and racing for his room with only minutes to spare before dinner.

By the next morning, Alexander was in a fever of excitement. He had spent the night dreaming about galloping into battle or riding in triumph through Macedonia on the back of the black stallion. Inside the throne room the dealers took turns describing their young horses. Alexander stood behind a pillar, where no one noticed him. Popolos was the third to speak. The plump little dealer from Thessaly waved his arms around, almost jumping up and down with excitement as he described his horse.

"He is amazing, exceptional!" he boasted. "I have never seen a better horse in all my years of trading."

A murmur of amusement ran around the room. King Philip raised an eyebrow. "Didn't you say that last year?"

"If I did, it was because I hadn't seen Bucephalus yet," Popolos countered quickly. "He is as brave as a lion and as strong as an ox, as clever as an owl and as cunning as a fox—"

The king interrupted him. "All right, that's enough. We will see this marvel go through his paces on the plain. What price do you seek for him?"

The dealer rubbed his hands together nervously. "Bucephalus is a horse fit for a king, your majesty. Such a horse only comes along once in a lifetime. The best price I can give you—and it is only because you are such a great king, sir—is thirteen talents."

Once again the quiet of the room was shattered by laughter. King Philip shook his head. "I could buy twenty horses for that," he said. "Why would I spend that kind of money on one?"

Popolos wiped his forehead nervously. "I can assure you that it is a fair price, your majesty. He is a horse without equal!"

Alexander watched his father. It was a huge amount of money to spend. He knew that his father wouldn't buy Bucephalus unless he was truly exceptional. But Alexander longed to own him.

It seemed like an eternity until the last dealer had said his piece. They all proposed to amaze the king with the beauty, bravery, and intelligence of their horses. Still, Popolos' words lingered in Alexander's mind. A horse without equal . . .

At last, King Philip rose to his feet. "We will gather on the plain in an hour," he announced. "Let the dealers prepare their horses for the display."

Alexander closed his eyes and whispered a prayer to any gods that were listening. "Please let Bucephalus perform well. Let him be all that Popolos said he is."

As his father led his court down to the plain, Alexander tagged onto the end of the procession. The horses had been lined up in the afternoon sun. Their hooves shone with oil, their coats had been brushed until they gleamed, and their manes were neatly braided. Alexander ran his eyes up and down the line, looking for Bucephalus. There! The horse was the tallest in the line and drew everyone's attention. Then Alexander frowned. Foamy sweat had gathered on Bucephalus' gleaming flanks. He was edging backward, gazing down at where his own shadow lay on the ground in front of him. He looked nervous, Alexander thought with a pang of worry. What was wrong?

King Philip beckoned to Tyros and sent him over to Popolos. The head groom would ride the horse to test it for speed, obedience, and stamina. These were the essential qualities for a warhorse. A soldier had to be able to trust his horse since a mistake in battle could be fatal.

Tyros reached up to take hold of the bridle so that he could lead the horse forward. With a jerk and a roll of his eyes, Bucephalus pulled his head away. Tyros frowned and tried again. He tugged roughly on the bridle this time, fighting the young stallion. Bucephalus began to dance nervously, pulling back. The horses on both sides of him skittered away. The muscles bunched in the head groom's arms as he drew the horse out of the line. He led Bucephalus to the area directly in front of King Philip.

The horse stood with his head down, quivering. Something was clearly wrong. At a nod from the king, Tyros vaulted onto the horse's back and gathered the reins. Immediately, the horse plunged and reared. He arched his back wickedly and dropped his head as he came down to earth. Tyros went flying, landing in a heap on the dusty ground. Another groom grabbed the flapping reins and struggled to bring the horse under control. Tyros jumped to his feet, red with anger. Alexander's mouth was dry. His father looked fearful.

"Popolos!" he called. "You have wasted our time! This horse is vicious and unmanageable. Take it away."

The horse trader hurried to obey. A lump rose in Alexander's throat. Without hesitating, he stepped forward and shouted, "Wait!" He had an idea that might help Bucephalus. It was worth a try.

His father whipped around and glared at him. "Do you have something to contribute, my son?"

Alexander swallowed. The entire court was staring at him, and all of them looked as if they disapproved. When he spoke, his voice sounded thin and reedy. "Your majesty, you are losing a great horse because your men don't know how to handle him."

Philip gave a humorless laugh. "Are you saying that you know more than I do about horses? Or that you can manage a horse better than the best grooms in my stable?"

Alexander stood his ground. "I could manage this one better, I know." He didn't dare look in Tyros' direction.

Philip said coldly, "And if you can't? What price will you pay?"

Without pausing, Alexander answered, "I will give you the price of the horse."

The whole group burst into laughter and scattered applause. Alexander was relieved to see that his father was as amused as any of them. He nodded at his son. "I admire your spirit, my boy. You may try to ride this horse, if that is what you want."

Alexander walked out in front of the crowd. Tyros gave a short, mocking laugh as he passed him, but Alexander ignored it. If he was wrong, Bucephalus would be sold to someone else, and Alexander would never see him again. His legs shook and his stomach flipped over as he reached the horse, who was rolling his eyes and fidgeting. Alexander moved slowly toward his head and took hold of the bridle. He ran his hand over Bucephalus' shoulder again and again, feeling the circular brand that marked every horse bred in Thessaly. Gradually, the black stallion began to calm down.

"I understand," Alexander said soothingly. "You've been told that you have no equal. It must be frightening to see another horse that can do everything you can do." The horse tossed his head haughtily.

"You're smart, aren't you?" Alexander said. "But not that smart. Imagine being frightened of your own shadow!"

Gently, he turned around, guiding Bucephalus so that he faced the sun. The horse's shadow streamed away from his feet behind him—the other horse that had so alarmed him. Alexander leaned his head against the horse's side for a moment, praying for courage. Then he hauled himself into the saddle and gathered up the reins. He was trembling. What if he had made a mistake? What if he couldn't control the horse? His hands dropped, and he felt dizzy.

Bucephalus shook his head and snorted impatiently. Alexander came to his senses. It was as if all of his fears had melted away. He urged the horse forward, flattening himself against his neck.

The wind rushed past them, the ground flashing beneath Bucephalus' hooves as they raced toward the sun.

Alexander wanted the ride to go on forever, but eventually he turned the stallion, and they cantered back to where the king was waiting. The watching crowd broke into cheers and applause, roaring Alexander's name as if he was a true hero.

Alexander dismounted and buried his head against Bucephalus' neck, overcome with relief and joy. He heard footsteps behind him and then felt his father's arm around his shoulders. "My boy," the king said proudly, "with this horse, you will conquer the world."

A Different Kind of Pony

MATILDA WEBB

Suzie stole a glance at her watch. Anna had held court about her last riding lesson for a full 15 minutes.

"I've ridden a pony too," Suzie blurted out before she could stop herself.

Anna turned on her. "No, you haven't!"

"Yes, I have, last summer."

"Yeah, right!" Katy said, rolling her eyes.

"How many hands was it?" Anna demanded.

"Um . . . I can't remember."

Someone snickered.

"What color was is it? What kind of saddle did it have? Did it need a martingale?" Anna fired questions at her.

"I'm not sure," Suzie said as her cheeks started to burn.

"I knew it! Your dad couldn't afford it anyway." Anna stood up and signaled to the others to do so too. "Come on. Suzie Make-Believe's at it again. What was it you told us when your mom left? She'd won a cruise! Won a cruise! What a little liar you are."

"I did ride a pony," Suzie muttered, her fists clenched. "Last summer . . . at the fair."

"Oh . . ." Anna paused. "At the fair . . . At that feeble excuse for a carnival on the soccer field." And she bent down until her face was level with Suzie's. Anna spoke to her as if she was a baby. "And did you have a nicey-wicey time on the carousel on the dented pony with all its paint peeling off?"

Anna stepped back and laughed cruelly. The others joined in. "Well, the fair's due back soon," she continued, "so remember, gather the reins, and don't forget to grip with your knees so you don't fall off now, okay?" She motioned to the other girls, who turned together and marched off after her to another part of the playground.

Suzie sat very still. She squeezed her eyes tightly shut. She wouldn't cry this time.

So what if it was the pony on the carousel? She remembered standing there, watching the ride going around and around, hundreds of colored bulbs lighting up its brightly painted canopy. And there, rising up and down as the ride turned, was a shiny white pony with such a fiery orange mane and tail that it had seemed alive to her, with its red leather saddle and reins and bright metal stirrups.

She'd hung around at the fair until she found enough dropped dimes beneath the Giant Swing Boat to pay for a ride on the carousel. She handed them excitedly to the woman in the booth and clambered onto the pony before anyone else could. As the organ music piped up and the ride started to turn faster, she leaned forward in the stirrups to whisper in the pony's ear. She told it that they were galloping together through a silent, pine-scented forest, the only noise the muffled drumming of its hooves.

That was last June, so the fair was due back any day now. You never knew when, exactly. It just seemed to appear out of nowhere in the soccer field at the edge of town, stay for the weekend, and then disappear just as suddenly.

But as Suzie lay awake a few nights later, too hot to sleep in the stuffy June air, she knew for sure that the fair had arrived.

She hadn't heard any sounds of booths being hammered together or shouts as the Giant Swing Boat was erected, but still, she knew. And when she finally fell asleep, she dreamed that she was on her pony, searching the dense pine trees for a way into the forest.

In the morning, as usual, she had to help her father with the housework and the weekly trip to the Laundromat. But by late afternoon it was all done, and she could get away. He gave her a dollar and a hug.

She was out the door in a flash and raced all the way down their long street until she reached the supermarket at the edge of town. She crossed the strip of wasteland behind it and hurried out onto the soccer field.

And there it was, a small group of rides and trailers in the middle of the field, the ground around them already trampled and muddy. The smell of fried onions drifted over from a burger stand and made her mouth water. As she passed it, she touched the dollar bill in her pocket but kept walking.

It was hot and airless inside the trailer. Why didn't they ever open the door anymore? The pony couldn't understand it. He was propped up against one side of the trailer, one wide eye staring at a stack of metal poles. He wanted to get out. He wanted to be set on his pedestal so that he could start going around and around like before. He enjoyed giving rides to children. Not the ones that picked at the flaking orange paint on his mane or

the ones who kicked him so hard in his stomach that they dented his sides. Just the ones who laughed and waved to their parents and stroked his neck—and especially the girl who'd seemed to understand that he was more than a toy.

There it was! Suzie ran forward. It hadn't taken long to find the carousel. As she looked for it, even she had to admit that the fair was a fairly small and shabby one. She hadn't noticed last year or the year before that.

But she stopped in confusion. Why wasn't the carousel all lit up? It stood slightly apart from the other rides at the far edge of the fair, and no one seemed to be around to operate it. She walked all around it, but there was no sign of the pony. Some of the other animals were missing too, and only a few of the sit-in boats and planes were still there. Most of the lightbulbs were smashed, and pieces of the canopy hung down in tatters.

Turning, Suzie saw someone throw his French fries onto the ground, and suddenly the fair lost all of its magic for her. Hands in her pockets, she tramped back through the other rides to the burger stand.

Taking small bites to prolong the delight of the burger, melted cheese, and onions, she wandered through the booths. Suddenly, Suzie recognized the woman who'd operated the carousel last summer. She was standing in the middle of a booth where you fished yellow plastic ducks out of the water with a magnet for one dollar a turn. She had a long pole with a hook at the end and was lifting down small pink teddy bears for those who'd succeeded.

Suzie went up and stood against the rail.

"One dollar, honey."

"Um, I don't want to play, thanks. I just want to know why the carousel isn't working anymore."

"She's gotten too old and rusty, honey. Just like me!" And she laughed heartily as she turned to get down another teddy bear.

"Won't it ever go around again?"

"I doubt it! I had a real fondness for the thing an' all," she added, more to herself than to Suzie, and then moved away to help a little boy.

"But what about the pony?" Suzie called, with a tremor in her voice that made the woman stop and really pay attention to her. She came back over and leaned her weight on the pole. "The whole ride's got to be thrown out, darling. Pony an' all." Suzie clung to the rail. "But why's it still set up?"

"Makes the fair look bigger, don't it? But it's being replaced tomorrow, with a space shuttle simulator or something. That's the boss over there, arranging its delivery." She pointed the pole in the direction of two men standing beyond the booth, before turning to collect more money.

The men were nodding and shaking hands.

Suzie stared at them as she walked slowly away from the booth. But then she stopped. She felt compelled to turn around. The woman was standing right behind her.

"Full moon tonight, honey. Strange things can happen at an old fair like this when there's a full moon." And she winked at Suzie and turned back to work.

The narrow strips of light around the trailer door slowly dimmed. The little pony sighed. Another day had gone by, and they still hadn't put him on the carousel. He'd lost count of the days. Maybe they would do it tomorrow. Maybe they were keeping him hidden as a surprise. Maybe the girl would come again.

That night Suzie stood by her bedroom window. She'd watched the moon appear, big and round above the rooftops. Now she waited impatiently for the familiar sounds of her father turning off the TV and making his way to bed.

Eventually, holding her sneakers by the laces, she crept downstairs and carefully opened the back door. After pausing briefly to check that she hadn't disturbed her father, she slipped outside.

She'd never been out alone at night before. The moon seemed unnaturally bright. She felt a sense of anticipation more than fear. She pulled on her sneakers, opened the back gate, and scampered down the alley toward the street.

Out of breath from running all the way, she crossed the field more slowly and was suddenly aware of snatches of organ music on the light evening breeze.

What was that noise? The carousel's music! Maybe they were going to put him on it now. A shiver of excitement coursed through the pony. At last! He could run again—flare his nostrils at the wind, swish his tail, and flatten his ears back for a gallop. He gazed at the trailer door as it slowly opened.

Suzie crept past the trailers. The families who worked at the fair lived in them, but there was no sign of life. All of the curtains were closed, and the trailers lay in darkness.

Beyond them, in contrast, the carousel was lit up in a blaze of light from its multicolored bulbs, no longer smashed and missing. All of the objects and animals were back in place, and when she ran around it, she spied her pony.

But she cried out when she drew closer to it. It was dented in so many places! And rust had covered the dents like a rash. There were hardly any traces of the orange paint left, and the shiny white was gray with dust and oil. The red leather saddle was torn, and one of the stirrups was missing.

Suzie climbed onto the floor of the ride. She pulled out a tissue and tried to clean around the pony's eyes and mouth, but the tissue was soon too dirty to be of use. She wrapped her arms around the pony's neck and leaned her cheek against his cool metal mane.

And although there was nobody in the operating booth, the ride started to turn.

Suzie put her foot in the remaining stirrup and swung herself up. She looked anxiously over toward the trailers, but they were still dark and silent.

The ride turned slowly at first but then began to get faster.

Suzie gathered the reins and gripped with her knees, kept her heels down, and moved her weight slightly forward to prepare for the gallop.

Then she leaned down and whispered in the pony's ear.

The pony tossed his pure-white head. He turned one glistening brown eye to stare at her. Sitting back up, she watched in wonder as the pony started to grow. His legs lengthened, and when his hooves touched the floor, he rose from his pedestal and stood free. The short reins snapped and fell away with the

rest of the old leather bridle. The girth snapped, and Suzie edged back to let the remains of the saddle fall to the floor.

The pony pawed the floor, but he seemed to be waiting for something. Suzie stroked his warm neck and wound her fingers into his thick, fiery mane. She clamped her legs onto his flanks.

The organ music started to wind down. The carousel slowed to a halt.

And with another snort, the pony leaped down to the ground.

Full of joy, Suzie nudged the pony's sides, and they set off, slowly at first and then increasing speed to a gentle, rocking canter that made her feel completely safe. They passed the dark trailers, and this time she saw that one person was awake. The woman stood framed in the light of her trailer door, wearing a voluminous nightgown. She was waving good-bye.

And they cantered away from the fair, away from the stores at the edge of town, over the moonlit fields, until they found a path into the forest. Pine needles carpeted the ground, and together they galloped, the only noise the muffled drumming of the pony's hooves.

Madrigal's Melody

LOIS RUBY

Maybe liver and onions for breakfast is worse than being the new girl at school, but with the liver deal, people actually talk to you while you're getting it down. At school, everybody slides past me like I'm the sixth-grade ghost. I blend into the poster on the wall. "Bloom Where You Are Planted," it says. I've been blooming since school started two months ago. Look at my feet. Yep, roots are growing—no kidding.

I know why they ignore me. Because I'm a Harbor House girl. Being homeless is as contagious as chicken pox, they think, and maybe it is. It's my first experience in a shelter. Better be my last, too.

So, I usually gaze out the window, and nothing ever happens out there. That's why I bolted out of my chair when a horse came trotting up to school, with a policewoman perched high and straight in the saddle. I opened the window to watch the horse nose its way into the gym.

"Geraldine!" Mrs. Halpern barked. I've told her a skillion times that I like "Gerri" better. "Geraldine, close the window and take your seat at once." They all laughed.

What was a horse doing in the gym? Well, I found out when the bell rang and we swarmed down there for a special assembly. Everyone else traipsed up to the bleachers, but I hit the floor—because that stallion stood right in front of me, huge and proud.

Sheesh, what if he needed to go in the middle of the assembly?

The police officer held his reins loosely. "Sergeant Karen Wendt," her badge said.

You know how noisy a gym is with a skillion kids whooping and wisecracking, so I had to yell. "Hey, what's your horse's name?"

Sergeant Wendt nudged the stallion closer to me. "It's Madrigal. I'll bet you don't know what a madrigal is." I shook my head. "It's a gentle, old-fashioned song. If you listen closely, you'll hear him singing. Want to try?"

Wow! Every Roosevelt eye was on me as I scrambled over and put my ear to the horse's throat. A tune rumbled up from him, a sound between a cat's purr and a scared dog's growl. Madrigal nosed me, glad I'd understood his song. I breathed in his fresh horsey smell, not a bit like manure, which you'd expect, or the sweaty dog at Harbor House that hadn't seen soap and water in a century.

Then—spooky—a picture flashed into my head. A younger Madrigal, clipping a hurdle as he tried to jump it. Suddenly, my leg throbbed something fierce, as if I'd banged it on the wooden rail myself, maybe cracked a bone. I clapped my hand to my shin, hopping around. They laughed. Then it hit me—I wasn't feeling my embarrassment—but Madrigal's, from when he was a colt. Weird. Shaking, I scurried back to the floor, feeling like I'd been zapped by lightning.

The principal hushed us and shouted into the mike about Sergeant Wendt being a member of the mounted police here to teach us Roosevelt Raiders about something or other, blah, blah, blah. Didn't matter what because now the assembly was about Madrigal and me, nobody else. His eyes never left me.

And me? I scanned every inch of his flank. His dark mane and tail were the exact same color as my own hair but lots neater. Plus, those legs seemed too spindly to hold up such a huge and magnificent creature.

Where was the hurt place on his shin from that day long ago? I spotted a circle where no hair grew below his left knee. One ear had a slight notch in it—from a fight? Bet the other horse looked worse. The right ear stood pert and straight. It took all my strength not to leap up and whisper into that ear—though what would I say? I sure wouldn't go *neigh*, like some idiot next to me did.

"Hello, Roosevelt Raiders!" Sergeant Wendt yelled, and the gym erupted like a volcano, until she raised her arm, and then all 600 kids fell silent. "How many of you ride a horse like Madrigal to school?"

Naturally, a couple of smart alecks raised their grubby hands.

"Lucky guys! But I'm guessing the rest of you walk, take the bus, or ride your bike, right? Well, I'm here to talk to you about bicycle safety . . ."

Madrigal looked bored while Sergeant Wendt's voice bounced off the padded walls. At the end, when everybody clapped, he dipped his head to take a bow, mocking the audience. We had a joke between us, Madrigal and me. He didn't like the Roosevelt Raiders any more than I did—no kidding.

Afterward, Sergeant Wendt called me over. "We're in Stanyan Park weekdays after school. Come by and visit us. Madrigal likes you." She nuzzled her face in the whorl of hair on his forehead, and dang if I didn't feel a stab of jealousy.

So, every afternoon that month, I patrolled the park with Madrigal and Sergeant Wendt. She sat up high, checking everything out, and Madrigal and I got to know each other down at his eye level.

He sang his life to me, and I told him all the things that I couldn't tell another living creature. "My dad left us," I whispered

into his ear. "Mom and I had no money." My face flushed red. "We live in a homeless shelter, just until Mom gets back on her feet." Madrigal sang *tell me more*. I did. Just by thinking thoughts, I told him every secret that'd been sticking in my heart like a thorny bundle of kindling. Madrigal snuggled under my arm and clopped his hoof to show that he understood me.

"This guy doesn't take to just anybody," Sergeant Wendt said, bending to my level. "You're special. Oh, rats, here comes that sorry pair again." She straightened up in the saddle. Her eyes followed the man with bleached hair who walked by every afternoon around four o'clock, yanking on the leash of the ugliest dog I ever saw. The first day I'd asked Sergeant Wendt, "What kind of dog is that thing?"

"Pit bull," she'd said, glaring at the mutt.

Madrigal didn't like the dog either. I felt his body tighten under my palm until the guy and his nasty mongrel disappeared around the gazebo.

"Mean dogs, those pit bulls," Sergeant Wendt muttered. "Don't worry. Madrigal's on the case."

But he wasn't. I knew he was scared, even if Sergeant Wendt was clueless.

I didn't remember clunking my ankle on a water pipe or anything last Monday, but it was hurting like the dickens, which griped me as I limped to the park after school.

Sergeant Wendt and Madrigal weren't there.

I checked the rain shelter, the gardener's shed, even the girls' bathroom, picturing Madrigal admiring himself in the mirror while Sergeant Wendt did her business in a stall. No sign of them anywhere.

They're stuck in a parade downtown, I thought. I curled up on a splintery bench to wait, shivering in the November frost and cradling my ankle. The air smelled heavy and cold. My nose ran, but I was so mad that I didn't care if the goop froze on my chin.

Where were they?

Hours passed. Snow feathered down. I drank snowflakes captured on my tongue. There was no one in the park but me and the trees with their bare arms raised up to the blue-black sky.

That night I figured out what "lonely" means. It's winter, it's dark, you're hurting, you're all by yourself, and no one's coming for you.

My fingers and toes were icicles ready to snap like dry twigs as I trudged back to Harbor House like I was dragging a ball and chain on my ankle.

"Good grief, Gerri, it's as dark as midnight," Mom cried. "Where've you been?"

"Usual place. The park."

"I was worried sick. Here, I saved you a sandwich." She handed it to me and wrapped her arm around me. "You're shivering, baby. Let's get you something hot." She steered me toward the clattering pans in the kitchen. "Oh, some Karen person called, an adult." She showed me a scrap with a number scrawled across it slantwise.

"Gimme that!" I growled, snapping the note out of her hand.

"Gerri! What's gotten into you? Bad influences here. We've got to get our own place—and pronto," Mom sighed as I spun around to the hall phone. She'd better not catch me limping, or she'd have me waiting all night at the free clinic.

Peanut butter plastered the roof of my mouth as I jabbed in Sergeant Wendt's number like I was trying to kill the phone. What had gotten into me?

Sergeant Wendt sounded spacey. "Oh, Gerri, yeah. It's about Madrigal."

He's dead! The bottom dropped out of my heart like an elevator plunging to the basement.

And then I knew he wasn't dead because I felt the pain pounding through him like a steady Indian drumbeat—not just in my ankle, all over.

"Gerri? You with me? You know that miserable so-and-so pit bull? Well, he broke loose and bit Madrigal's leg clear to the bone. Threw me off, but I'm bruised and sore, that's all. Could have been lots worse."

Tears sprang to my eyes, and I never cry. "Is he okay?"

"The vet's treated the bite, but Madrigal's facing lots of medication and wound dressing. When the swelling goes down, he'll need stitches. Our baby's pretty bad off, Gerri. He could use a friend."

Me!

"You and Madrigal seem to sing the same tunes," Sergeant Wendt said. "Can you come by the stable tomorrow after school? Let me talk to your mother. If she says it's okay, I'll pick you up in an unmarked car."

"Mom!" I cried and handed over the phone.

I could smell Madrigal's hurt as soon as I hit the stable. The other horses pointed me toward him before Sergeant Wendt opened the gate for me and respectfully stood outside the stall.

Oh! Madrigal lay in a cradle of hay, strapped down, with his thick bandaged leg propped up on a tacky pillow.

"Something's wrong with his eyes," I murmured. They were as dull as dust, with the lids fluttering weakly.

Sergeant Wendt said, "He gets pain shots every three hours. It's hard for him to stay awake."

He perked up when I plopped down in the prickly hay beside him, stroking his head, his ears, his tight, muscular shoulders. I fed him a handful of hay, which he ate just to please me. And he sang.

His song was as sad as one of those country-and-western numbers about some guy losing his girl to his best buddy. It's hard to say what Madrigal told me that day, at least in words, but I know that he was glad I was there to ease his pain. Besides, he was spitting mad at that vicious mutt.

I was too, but lying in that hay, I was starting to feel like a real whole person, not a Harbor House girl, 'cause, no kidding, home isn't about four walls. It's about being where somebody you love hangs out.

Madrigal drifted off to sleep, and I sat with him for an hour or two until the vet came to give him another shot. I couldn't watch—just couldn't.

On the way home in the police car Sergeant Wendt asked me, "What did Madrigal tell you? For years we've been as close as human and beast can be, but he doesn't talk to me like he does to you. Truth is, Gerri, I'm a little jealous."

I clammed up. What do you say when an adult treats you—well, like an adult?

"It's all right," she assured me, but I noticed that she clenched the steering wheel and bit her lip.

We were almost at Harbor House before I found the words. "He likes you a lot, Sergeant Wendt. Honest. He'd give his life for you."

She smiled at me with watery eyes. "I know."

A month's passed. Madrigal and Sergeant Wendt are back on duty. Don't ask me what happened to the pit bull, but he deserved it— no kidding. Also, Mom's starting a job at the old folk's home near Stanyan Park. We're going to rent a one bedroom with a microwave. "Lap of luxury," Mom says.

Things are looking up at Roosevelt, too. I'm not Queen of the Sixth Grade, but now a couple of horse girls bring their lunch trays over by me and ask about Madrigal, so it's a start. I guess Sami and Janine are my friends, but they'd think I was a loony-toon if they knew that Madrigal talks to me as plain as day, so I keep my mouth zipped about that and just say *he's getting stronger, thanks for asking, and isn't the ham casserole yuckier than usual today?*

The truth is, Madrigal and me are best buddies. We can gab away about anything and everything, without a sound cracking the silence between us. We understand each other's hearts and feel each other's hurts. That's what best buddies do—no kidding!

The Parking Lot Pony

JUDY PATERSON

Everyone called him the Parking Lot Pony. He was hairy the way Shetland ponies usually are and jet-black. His long mane fell on both sides of his neck, his tail touched the ground, and he had the biggest, softest eyes in the world. He was the first pony I ever rode.

He was kept tethered on the grass beside the parking lot at the little riding school on the edge of town. Old Mrs. Wilson owned the school. She had a few other ponies. She taught the local children to ride. They all started off on the Parking Lot Pony.

"That's the way he earns his keep," she used to say.

One magic day, just after my fourth birthday, Mrs. Wilson came out to meet Mom and me carrying the pony's saddle and lead rope.

"Well, Amy, your mom told me you're going to ride Ben," she said.

She probably said lots of other things, but I heard nothing more. I was going to ride the Parking Lot Pony! I stood beside him, stroking his warm nose and looking into his big, soft eyes. Suddenly, I was lifted up, and there I was on his back. I grabbed two fistfuls of his mane, and Mrs. Wilson led me around the parking lot. I can still feel his thick mane in my hands, the strange sensation of being carried on his sturdy back, the soft clop of his unshod hooves, and the horrible realization when, all too soon, the ride was over and I was being lifted off. I cried.

Mrs. Wilson was concerned. "Oh, dearie, were you frightened?" But I couldn't explain why I was crying. I didn't know how to say that I was so happy but also so sad that it was over.

When Dad came home, I was full of myself. "I rode the Parking Lot Pony. His real name is Ben, and can I ride him again, please?"

Dad smiled. "Having rides costs money, you know, and we are saving up for the baby!"

"Baby can have my toys," I offered generously, and Dad laughed.

So that was the start of my life with horses.

Mrs. Wilson was a crusty sort of person on the surface, and anyone riding her ponies had to know how to care for them too.

"No such thing as a free ride," she'd say, and I thought that this was amusing since Mom always paid for my lessons. Even the youngest of us helped by brushing the parts we could reach before we went riding. Little by little, as I got older, I learned about the tack and how to put on a bridle and a saddle. I loved the smell of it all—the warm, hairy smell of the horses and the polished scent of leather. Best of all was taking care of Ben. He always greeted me with a little whinny and stood patiently as I groomed him and picked out his feet.

When Gran was young, she used to ride. She had an amazing collection of cups and ribbons. She bought my first jodhpurs, long riding boots, and safety helmet. She always loved hearing about my progress on Ben when she came to visit.

"Sounds like a special pony, that one!" she said, and I agreed.

Soon I was riding all by myself, and I felt as if there was no one else in the whole world but that pony and me. But I had to share him with everyone else my age, and sometimes taking turns was very difficult. I felt like Ben was my pony—at least, I wished he was.

So I began to nag Mom and Dad. By this time my little sister had come along, and I thought that I had the perfect argument.

"Please, may I have a pony? If I have a pony, then I can teach Emily to ride when she's big."

"And where will you keep it?" Mom asked, laughing. "In the bedroom?"

She was right. We lived in a small house in the middle of a busy town, and having a pony was just a dream.

Before too long, however, my dream was to ride the bigger ponies, like the older girls. One day Mrs. Wilson called to me while I was grooming Ben.

"Amy, you are getting too big for him. Come over here, and we'll see how you do with Fleur."

I flung the brush into the tack box and almost tripped over as

I raced across the yard. Fleur was a beautiful palomino, with a coat of pale sunshine. Her mane and tail were the color of moonlight. Fleur and I got on famously from the start. Then, when I grew again and had learned even more, I rode Cherokee, the skewbald pony, and finally I rode Sandy, who was gray, the color of clouds touched by the sun.

Sandy was a real character. He was spunky, got his nose into everything, and he thought the best time for a roll in the mud was just before a ride. I learned to trust him as much as I trusted Ben, and we started to go to pony-club gymkhanas and win prizes.

I enjoyed leading smaller children around on the Parking Lot Pony. I would tell them his real name and show them how to groom him. I loved watching their little faces light up when they sat on Ben's back, and of course I enjoyed being "the big girl." I felt grown-up, even though I was only 11. However, the best thing was being with my wonderful Ben. I learned to appreciate what a rare and gentle nature he had.

"I don't know what I'd do without you, Amy," Mrs. Wilson said one day. "I'm not as young as I used to be. I suppose one day I'll have to give up."

I was stunned. "What would we do without you?"

"Well, it won't be tomorrow, dearie. I'm a tough old stick, you know."

But it weighed on my mind. I discussed it with Mom at bedtime.

"Where would we ride? What would happen to the ponies? Why would she give up?" I asked.

"Calm down!" Mom said. "Mrs. Wilson is an old lady, sweetheart, and maybe she'd like to retire and take a rest. We'd find another place for you to have lessons."

"I like Mrs. Wilson—and having lessons on *her* ponies," I said glumly.

"Amy, Mrs. Wilson is going to be around for a good long while

yet. So stop worrying."

I didn't sleep very well that night. Old people often got tired. Even my gran complained sometimes about living so far out of town. I suppose I never really thought about Mrs. Wilson being old.

In the morning the sun was shining, and I decided to walk to school early so that I could see the ponies. Mrs. Wilson was mucking out and gave me a cheery wave. I watched her pitch more dirty straw onto the mountain that was already in the wheelbarrow. Sandy was chasing Cherokee around the field, and Ben whinnied. I stroked his nose and was happy again.

Then, a few weeks later, Mom and Dad started talking about moving.

"This house is just too small, darling," Dad said one Saturday morning. "You'll be in junior high soon. You'll need a room of your own."

"When are we going?" I asked in alarm. "Where to?"

"We have to find the right place first," he replied, and that was the end of that conversation.

I went up to the bedroom that I shared with Emily, but she was cutting out pictures and making a real mess. Outside, it was raining, and the black clouds said it would rain all day. No riding today. I sighed and slumped onto my bed, scattering Emily's cutouts everywhere.

"Mom!" Emily wailed.

I knew what to do. Grabbing my jacket and boots, I ran downstairs and said I was going to the stable.

"In this weather?" Mom shouted after me.

"Cleaning tack," I shouted back.

As soon as I arrived at the yard, I knew something was wrong. The ponies were stamping, and I could see that they hadn't been fed. I started to walk to Mrs. Wilson's house, and that's when I found her. She was lying on the grass in the pouring rain.

"Call an ambulance," she said weakly.

The rest of the morning went by in a blur. I covered her with a horse blanket and sat with her until the ambulance arrived. Then I called Mom and Dad.

"I'm getting some of the girls down to help," I said. "We have to take care of the ponies."

So we did. We worked in silence, all of us too stunned to talk. In the late afternoon Mrs. Wilson's daughter arrived after a long journey from her home and visiting the hospital.

"I was told you girls would have things under control here. Thank you so much." She pulled out her purse and gave each one of us a crisp new five-dollar bill. We gathered around her in disbelief.

"Is Mrs. Wilson all right?" I asked. "When will she come home from the hospital?"

"She's broken her hip and will need a long time to recuperate," she replied. "This had been getting too much for her, so we've decided to sell everything. She'll get a lot of money for this land. They want it for a supermarket, you know."

We looked at each other, understanding what that meant. This was the end of our little riding school. It was still raining, and I cried all the way home.

"It's not the end of the world," Dad said.

"It's the end of *my* world," I sobbed.

The "For Sale" signs went up that week, and we were told that the ponies would be sold to good homes. I went down every afternoon after school to help out, but it was hard. I worried at night. Where would the ponies go?

In the middle of all of this Mom tried to talk to me. "We've found the right house, Amy, and with all of the changes going on, a move will be the best thing."

But I wasn't interested. I didn't even ask where it was. When Mrs. Wilson came home from the hospital, I went to visit her. I was shocked to see her looking so pale and thin.

She smiled. "Amy, tell me what's been going on."

So I sat and told her how everyone had helped and how sad we were that she was leaving, and then I burst into tears. I couldn't tell her how worried I was about the ponies and how much I'd miss them.

"Shh, dearie," she said, and to my astonishment, she laughed. "You've worked so hard and been so good and kind at home that you should have one of the ponies."

"But how? Where? I mean, I can't keep him in our backyard!" I blurted out.

"How about this new house of yours? I've heard that you're going to live in your gran's house in the country, and she is coming to live in your house in town."

I didn't know what to say. I just sat there. A pony of my own!

"Now, Amy, you go out and talk to all those ponies and see which one you want for your very own."

So I did. I went to each pony. I knew them so well. My heart was pounding. As I stroked each one, I remembered my first jump on Fleur, the ribbon I won on Cherokee. When I went back to Mrs. Wilson, Mom and Dad were there.

"Well?" asked Mrs. Wilson.

"Sandy is the best choice because he's the biggest, so I can ride him even when I'm in high school," I said. "He's so much fun."

"Sensible girl," said Mrs. Wilson. "Lucky Sandy."

"No," I whispered, but I really meant it. "I want to take little Ben—because he was the first pony I ever rode. He's spent all of his life earning his keep, and I think he deserves a rest. And I can teach Emily how to ride him. I love that pony."

"Well, well," was all Mrs. Wilson said.

We moved into Gran's house a month later, and I couldn't wait for Ben to arrive. I could hardly believe that he would be mine at last.

When the door of the trailer opened, Sandy ambled out.

"No, that's not right," I said. "He's the wrong one!"

Mom laughed. So did Dad. Then out came my wonderful shaggy black friend, and I couldn't say a word.

"We thought Ben would need a friend, Amy—one that you can ride."

I stroked Sandy's nose. Then I wrapped my arms around Ben's neck. Running my hands over his thick mane, I whispered in his velvety ear, "You'll never be a Parking Lot Pony again."

Little Miss Perfect and Me

REBECCA KRAFT RECTOR

Mountain laurels and pine trees lined the trail, filling the air with sweet scents. The best smell of all, of course, was the smell of a horse. I leaned forward in the saddle and buried my face in Valiant's chestnut neck.

Valiant flicked an ear back at me. The steady thud of his hooves on the dirt didn't change rhythm. He liked it when I hugged him. When I was on the ground, instead of in the saddle, he rested his head on my shoulder. I figured that was the same as a horse hug.

"You're the best horse in the whole world!" I sat up and smoothed his mane, admiring the way a ray of sunlight made the golden hairs glisten. "I love being with you because I can leave everything else behind."

I especially loved leaving my bossy new stepsister behind. Charlotte was 13, two years older than me. For two weeks now she'd followed me around, telling me what to do. "Brush your hair like this." "Have you done your math homework yet?" "You can't wear that shirt to school!"

The only time I was safe from her bossiness was when I was with Valiant. She'd never followed me to Morningstar Stables, where he was boarded. Probably afraid she'd get dirt on her designer jeans.

Suddenly, Valiant's ears swiveled, and I felt his muscles tighten under me.

"Wait, Lucy!" someone shouted.

It couldn't be.

Sticks cracked, and leaves rustled behind us. I turned Valiant so that he could see what was coming. He waited alertly, head up, ears pricked forward. A moment later Charlotte pedaled a bicycle around the curve in the trail. Her dark green blouse matched the dark green bow at the top of her neat ponytail. Little Miss Perfect.

"I brought your camera," she called. "I should have brought you a long-sleeved shirt so your arms don't get scratched by all these branches."

I gritted my teeth. To think I'd been happy when Mike married my mother and Charlotte moved in with us. A big sister! Someone to talk to and share secrets with—maybe someone to help me with the barn chores.

But instead of my dream sister, I got Charlotte.

Valiant snorted nervously as the bike came closer. I stroked his neck and glared at Charlotte. "You're making my horse nervous."

I was happy to see the camera, though. I'd been in such a hurry to get away from Charlotte that I'd left it at home. It was a present from Mike, my new stepfather.

"I want lots of pictures of my two girls," Mike had said. "Take pictures of each other."

I liked Mike. I liked the camera. I planned to take lots of pictures. Of Valiant.

Charlotte bumped over the trail, closer and closer to us.

Valiant turned his hindquarters toward the bicycle, and I knew that he was thinking about running. I sat heavy and deep in the saddle. "Easy, there," I said, keeping a soft touch on the reins. "It's just horrible Charlotte. The one I'm NOT sharing you with."

It was hard enough sharing my mother—seeing Mom smiling

at Charlotte, telling her how nice she looked, cooking her pancakes when she knew that I liked waffles better.

"I never asked to share your horse," Charlotte said as she approached. "But your mom thought it would be nice if I visited you at the barn."

I didn't believe it. Mom wouldn't do that to me. Would she?

But I didn't have time to think about it now. Valiant danced sideways, trying to get away from the bicycle. Mountain laurels jabbed at us, and Valiant spurted forward down the trail.

"Wait for me," Charlotte shouted.

I wanted to get away from Charlotte, but this trail was too narrow and rough for cantering. I squeezed the reins, and Valiant obediently dropped back to a slow trot. A small branch lay in our path. Valiant took it in his stride.

But Charlotte didn't.

"Ow!" she howled.

I glanced back.

Charlotte, the broken branch, and the bike lay tangled together.

My stomach felt hollow, and my heart started beating fast. I turned Valiant and urged him toward Charlotte. He hesitated when he saw the spinning front wheel, but he trusted me enough to walk closer. "Charlotte?"

"Get this thing off me," Charlotte grumbled.

I breathed a sigh of relief and slid out of the saddle. I gripped Valiant's reins with my left hand and pulled at the bike with my right. Valiant tried to back away when the bike moved, but I soothed him.

"Don't let him step on me," Charlotte said, scrambling to her feet and snatching up the camera. "This looks okay."

At least she wasn't a crybaby. "Your hand is bleeding." Little red droplets welled up across the back of her hand.

Charlotte pulled a tissue from her pocket and dabbed at the blood. "I'll have to wash it when we get back to the barn. You have soap and water there, don't you?"

Hadn't she ever been in a barn before?

"Of course we do. How else would we take care of the horses?" Then I felt guilty. "I'll show you where the hose is, and I'll even let you use some of Valiant's antiseptic ointment."

"You want me to use horse medicine and water out of a hose?" Charlotte sounded like I'd suggested using rattlesnake venom.

I rolled my eyes and got back on my horse. "We'll go back to the barn, but you have to go first. Valiant doesn't like the bike behind him."

"What if he tries to run me down?" Charlotte stared at Valiant's hooves.

"He's not going to run you down!"

With a last worried look, Charlotte pedaled away.

Valiant settled into his usual long-striding walk. He didn't mind the bicycle now, as long as he could see it.

When we got back, I slid out of the saddle, and Charlotte propped up her bike against the barn.

"Come on, Charlotte," I said.

Charlotte eyed the shadowy doorway as if she expected lions and tigers and bears to come out. "I'll wait here."

She was probably afraid that she'd get dirty. "Whatever."

I took my time putting away my tack and currying Valiant. When his golden coat was gleaming, I shoved the antiseptic into my pocket, grabbed the bag of carrots, and led him out.

Charlotte flattened herself against the side of the barn.

"Here," I said, holding out the antiseptic.

She didn't move. "Why don't you put Valiant in the field first?"

She couldn't be afraid of horses, could she? No, that was ridiculous. She was just being bossy, as usual.

In the field I gave Valiant some carrots and slipped off his halter. He rested his head on my shoulder. "I have to do my barn chores now," I told him with a hug. "See you later."

He trotted down the field to join the three bay lesson ponies grazing near the fence. I loved the way that the sun sparkled on his chestnut coat and the way his full tail swished around his legs. Valiant was worth every smelly barn chore that I had to do to keep him.

"Lucy!" Charlotte called. "Where's that ointment?"

I found Charlotte washing her hands with the outside hose. She took the ointment from me and smoothed it over the cut.

I pulled the camera from her bike basket. "Valiant," I called, going back to the gate. "Come get your picture taken."

Behind me, Charlotte laughed. "You act like he can understand—"

Valiant looked up at the sound of my voice and started walking toward the gate.

"Well, would you look at that." Charlotte stood at my shoulder. "Does Valiant always come when you call?"

I beamed. "What can I say? He loves me."

Charlotte shook her head. "This is an example of animal training. He gets rewarded when he does something right. You call, he comes, he gets fed. He doesn't love you—he loves your carrots."

"Does not!"

"Does too!"

Valiant reached the gate and stretched to nuzzle my shoulder.

"Give me those carrots. I'll show you what he loves." Charlotte grabbed them and walked along the fence line. She ducked between the boards and went into the pasture. I grinned when I saw the big patch of dirt on her backside.

"Valiant! Here, Valiant!" Charlotte called.

Valiant's ears flicked back and forth at the noise, but he didn't move away from me. "Get over here, Valiant!"

I went through the gate and carefully closed it behind me. I gave Valiant a quick hug and marched over to Charlotte. "Don't tell my horse what to do. You don't know anything about horses and—"

Charlotte looked over my shoulder and screamed. "Look out! He's going to run us over!" She ran back to the fence and slid through. She got more mud on her jeans, but she didn't even notice.

Valiant walked up beside me, and I patted him absently.

"What's the matter with you?" I called. "He's just following me."

"Valiant! Look, carrots! Come here, Valiant!"

Valiant's ears flicked toward the arm sticking boldly out of the fence. He sniffed delicately and walked over to investigate.

"Aww, Valiant," I said. "Why do you have to be so curious?" I followed as he stretched his nose to Charlotte. She was holding out a carrot with the tips of her fingers.

"Charlotte!" I ran over and grabbed the carrot. "You can't do it that way. Your hand has to be flat." Didn't she know anything?

I broke the carrot into pieces and gave them to Valiant.

"Lucy, let me do it. You'll see. He loves anyone with carrots." Charlotte stuck her hand out flat, with a piece of carrot on it. When Valiant lowered his nose, her arm shook, and her fingers started to curl up.

Charlotte was afraid!

"Make your fingers flat, Charlotte."

Her fingers became rigid, and Valiant's lips lifted the carrot off of her hand.

"It didn't hurt!" Charlotte said.

"Of course not!" Why'd she follow me to the barn if she was so afraid of horses?

"His nose is soft." Charlotte gave Valiant another piece of carrot.

I smiled. At least she appreciated Valiant.

Valiant leaned over the fence to sniff Charlotte's pockets and blew in her hair. Charlotte stood very still. While he chewed on another piece of carrot, Charlotte slowly slid through the fence and patted his neck.

"He likes it better if you stroke him," I told her. "Like a cat— nice, long strokes."

Charlotte hesitated and then lightly stroked his neck.

I didn't mind teaching Charlotte how to make friends with Valiant. Valiant deserved lots of friends, and it didn't look as if she'd want to ride him. But Charlotte needed to understand one thing.

"Valiant likes your carrots," I said, "but it's *me* he loves."

"Is not," Charlotte said. She smoothed the funny spot on Valiant's forehead where the hair grew crooked.

"Is so," I said, rubbing Valiant's ears.

"I forgive you for trying to run me over," Charlotte whispered to Valiant.

"He didn't try to run you over! I told you—"

"Just don't do it again, and we can be friends." Charlotte gave Valiant another carrot chunk.

I groaned. She was hopeless.

"Now, what do I have to do to be friends with Lucy?" she asked Valiant.

I stared.

Charlotte didn't look at me. She just kept feeding Valiant carrots. "What if I promise not to run her over? And I'll feed her carrots when she's good."

I laughed. I couldn't help it.

"Maybe I could help her shovel out stalls." Charlotte didn't smile, and she still didn't look at me.

She was afraid of horses, but she followed me to the barn.

I swallowed and found my voice. "Stalls are smelly and dirty. You'll hate it."

Charlotte straightened Valiant's forelock. Then she finally looked at me.

"Maybe. But I can try, if you tell me what to do."

Me? Tell Charlotte what to do? Boss her around?

Charlotte had lost her little green bow, her jeans were muddy, and even her shirt was stained where Valiant had sniffed her. She didn't look like Little Miss Perfect anymore. She looked—well, she looked like me. Dirty. Messy. And she smelled like a horse.

"I want to get a picture of Valiant." I raised the camera and focused. Valiant nudged Charlotte, and suddenly they were both in the frame. I hesitated and then took a picture of my horse—and my new big sister.

Inkblack

A Tale From Medieval Japan

ROSEMARY CHIBA

A most unusual thing happened before dawn that day. I was fast asleep in Inkblack's stall when there was a commotion outside. Several riders had arrived unexpectedly. I jumped up as the stable doors were flung wide-open to the freezing air, and exhausted horses were brought inside to be fed and rubbed down with straw. Inkblack reached out to sniff them with interest.

Elder Sister soon came looking for me, knowing that when I have nightmares, I often go to Inkblack and doze off next to him. She seized my sleeve and pulled me to the kitchen, complaining, "It's disgraceful, the daughter of the house sleeping in the stable!"

She's not really my sister. She's the young wife of my eldest brother. These days she treats me more like a servant. She ordered me to fetch water from the well, wash the rice, and then scrub long white radishes in the icy stream outside.

"Are these guests Lord Fujiwara's men?" I asked her. I thought that perhaps they had come to buy my father's horses again.

As she bustled out of the kitchen, Elder Sister replied severely, "No one's to ask any questions—you least of all."

I bit my lip and picked up the water bucket.

"Take no notice," said the cook, a kind old woman who often took my side. She heaved an enormous pot of rice onto an earthen oven and then wiped her sooty face. "Remember how meek and mild she was when your mother was alive? Mark my words, she's a fox in disguise!"

Our valley is full of such strange old tales. I imagined a bushy tail showing beneath Elder Sister's kimono and giggled.

Whoever they were, the guests were important. They had been shown into the best room in the other wing of our L-shaped house and were talking to my father. Every time people came, I feared that they would try to buy Inkblack, even though my father had promised me that he would never sell him.

Often I would be sent to wait on guests, but this morning Elder Sister insisted on carrying in the lacquered bowls full of steaming soup herself. She knelt to slide open the painted door and bowed deeply before entering, but she soon came out with her perfect lips pursed.

As she passed me, she snapped, "There is still straw in your hair, and you smell like horses." Then she pinched my cheek as if I was a small child. I dodged away from her, ran to the everyday entrance, and stepped down into a pair of wooden clogs. In the outdoor bathroom I poured water from the bamboo dipper to cool my red, stinging face.

The sun had just risen above the mountains in the east and was streaming down the length of our valley. Everywhere, plants were sending out green shoots, and a few days before, the long, trailing branches of the ancient weeping cherries had burst into bloom. Already a breeze was scattering showers of petals onto the thatched roof and across the stones.

I breathed deeply. My father says that there are two ways to make you feel calm. "Either you can gaze at our beautiful valley of Tono, protected by its sacred mountains, or," and here his eyes always twinkle, "you can run your hand down the neck of a perfect horse and across its smooth back."

How fortunate I was! Inkblack was the perfect horse, and this was my home.

I heard Inkblack whinnying. He had smelled the spring air too and longed to be outside again. All of us, people and animals, had been shut up together in the house for the long winter months while heavy snow closed off the valley. Our storehouses were full of food, but the deeper the snow drifted outside, the higher the tempers rose inside.

Catching sight of my father, I called out happily, "Can I bring Inkblack out into the sunshine later on to groom him?"

But he had gone before I finished my request.

I frowned. My father had always been very indulgent of me, the youngest child, especially after my elder brothers and sisters married and moved away. I was born in the Year of the Horse and he called me his "little foal." How could he not? His entire life revolved around horses.

I remember sitting on his knee one winter night. He told me how our horses had originally come from a great kingdom across the sea, where they ran for days and days across endless grassy plains. I couldn't imagine such a vast country.

Even without being cut off for half the year, our mountain valley is remote. The only reason outsiders come here is for our horses, which are the most highly prized in all of Japan. Thanks to the mighty Fujiwara family, Father says, the northeast region is peaceful, but elsewhere battles rage, and warhorses are in endless demand.

My father is the most famous breeder of all. Among horses, he is so calm, like the eye of a summer typhoon. Unbroken horses whirl around him until he patiently teaches them to understand what he is asking of them. In turn, he respects their power and beauty. He can always see the true character of a horse. He told me, "My horses will be tested to the limit and must trust their riders in the battles of men."

Inkblack was a warhorse. I shuddered to think what he must have endured.

"I hate it too, little foal," my father said, "but that is the way of the world."

I didn't want to go back inside on such a glorious morning, but my chores were endless. By midmorning, the guests were resting, and in the kitchen the servants took a welcome break. As they sipped tea, they whispered secrets. They claimed that one guest was a famous general. I imagined a grim man who rode his horses into terrible wars without caring about them.

I slipped back to the stables in the west wing. Inkblack snickered when he caught sight of me.

"Oh, so now you want my attention!" I teased him and pretended to be more interested in the tired new horses. Most were dozing on their feet, but one mare was moving restlessly.

I discovered my father crouching beside her, rubbing her leg with warm oil and herbs.

"Is she hurt, Father?"

He nodded. "Lame in her right foreleg. She missed her footing in the dark."

I made a face. Surely this was the fault of her rider—maybe that grim old general—traveling in such conditions. I muttered, "Poor horse."

My father read my thoughts. "Sometimes men must take desperate measures. This horse's rider has always dared to do what no others would attempt. He is the bravest of warriors but now . . ." He suddenly checked himself like a man pulling hard on a rein.

I stroked the injured animal, but by now Inkblack was jealous and snorting his disapproval.

"Oh, you wicked Inkblack!" I laughed as I ducked beneath the boards and hugged him.

Inkblack came to us when I was still small. He had been badly injured in a battle, but my father slowly nursed him back to health, confident that he would give us many fine foals. For safety, I was warned to stay clear of the great, black horse with his feathered legs. Though healed, his old wounds still troubled him sometimes, and he could be bad tempered. One day, however, I sat down in his stall and sang to him. Inkblack nuzzled my hair. It tickled, and I put up my arms to kiss his soft muzzle. That's when my amazed father discovered us. Since then he has been the gentlest horse in our stable and my dearest friend.

Elder Sister always takes a nap after lunch. I led Inkblack outside and tied him beneath the cherries. I still only reached as high as his shoulder, so I had to stand on a box to brush him and pluck out the matted clumps of dusty winter hair. It was hard work, but gradually his black coat began to glow with a deep richness, like the 30 layers of lacquer on our wooden bowls. Inkblack stared intently down into the valley, with his ears pricked, twitching them whenever a shower of cherry petals fell.

"You're thinking of our rides in the forest!" I said, leaning my aching arms across his broad back. Sometimes he had to help haul wood. While the woodcutters were at work, we would ride through the trees. Once we were set upon by a desperate pack of wolves, but Inkblack never flinched. He leaped right over the leader and outran the pack.

I was dreaming like this when one of the guests, around the same age as my brother, approached Inkblack and offered him a cake of sweet bean paste. "A fine horse!" he said, stroking his muzzle. I liked him at once.

He said wistfully, "I had a horse just like this. He was called Valiant Black. We were in a terrible battle. The enemy was fighting on the beach, and we had to find a way down an almost sheer cliff to attack them by surprise. My horse was so fearless that he inspired all of the others to follow."

"Did you win the battle?"

"We did—and others—but in the end we lost everything." He sighed and turned back to the house.

When I led Inkblack inside, my father was waiting by his stall. "Little foal," he said gently, and my heart missed a beat. "That mare is still lame, and I must offer one of our horses."

"For the general? Not Inkblack, Father, please not!"

"Who has spoken of such matters?" my father demanded, more stern than I had ever seen him.

I hung my head.

My father's anger passed, but he was still fearful. "The general has been hunted by his own half brother and betrayed by his hosts. People I trusted."

I could not follow this, nor did I want to. All I knew was that a horrible old general would climb up onto my beloved horse and ride him away. I would never see Inkblack again.

With tears streaming down my face, I pleaded with my father, but it was no use.

"The general must travel in the utmost secrecy, and his journey may take many months. Only a horse as strong and dark as Inkblack could carry the general secretly by night to safety. It is the greatest honor that a horse of ours could ever have."

I turned to Inkblack and buried my wet face in his silky neck. Troubled by my unhappiness, he trembled and tried to twist around to touch me. My father called back softly, "Don't forget, his next foal will be born this month."

No daughter can disobey her father. I reached for the brush and drew it for the last time through Inkblack's rippling mane and tail. He had to be as beautiful as possible when he left. Then I pulled a dark ribbon from my hair, let him sniff it, and braided it into his forelock.

"Remember me."

Much too soon, Elder Sister called shrilly for me to come and help. An evening meal must be served before the guests left again under the cover of darkness.

I managed to escape from the kitchen only just in time to see the riders mounting. My father was bowing right to the ground as the general thanked him.

I gasped. It was the young man who had spoken to me! Astride Inkblack, he looked magnificent.

"Where is the girl who groomed this horse so well?"

I wiped away my tears and came forward. The general leaned down and asked kindly, "What is his name?"

The words would not come, but at last I replied, "Inkblack, my lord."

In the autumn, when the mountain maples were flaming with scarlet leaves, my father received a secret letter from the far north. There was only a short poem inside, brushed in black ink on the soft paper. He showed it to me:

no more din of war
the black horse runs free as wind
on the pampas moor

Ride Like the Wind

PAMELA KAVANAGH

Chantal ran blindly down the farm track, heading for the river path where she could be alone. Anything to get away from her brother's taunts and jibes. She knew Andre didn't mean to be unkind. He simply did not understand why, after spending all of her 12 years with horses, she could no longer bring herself to get on one. Chantal could not explain the fear that locked her limbs at the very thought of Jonti bolting with her, going faster and faster, and being powerless to stop him. Jonti was now turned out with the young stock. Still loved, yet not ridden. Mama and Papa told her not to worry, that riding didn't matter. Chantal knew that it did. The Boile farm, where Papa bred black Camargue cattle, was vast, the ground marshy and rough. How else could they get around if not on horseback?

Reaching the river, Chantal flung herself down on the bank with a sigh. She was a pretty girl with long, fair hair and big brown eyes that, at the moment, wore a troubled look. Suddenly, some movement in the reeds caught her attention. Struggling in the water was a small figure.

"Hold on!" Chantal shouted. Forgetting her own problems, she slipped into the shallows and waded to the rescue. She reached the child just as the current was about to sweep him away and dragged him back to the safety of the bank. He stood there, bedraggled and dripping—a gypsy boy, judging by his dark hair and the coal-black eyes that regarded her balefully from a thin brown face.

A cool breeze stirred the reeds and rippled the water, and Chantal shivered. "What's your name?" she asked.

The child did not answer. His bottom lip started to wobble.

"Don't cry," Chantal soothed, chafing his cold, wet hands. It was May, when the traveling people from all over the world came on pilgrimage to Saintes Maries de la Mer for the Festival of Sara, their patron saint. The boy would belong to one of these families. She smiled at him encouragingly. "Can you show me where your people are camped?"

To her relief, he pointed toward a distant grove of pine trees, where a plume of wood smoke was rising. They set off, the child trotting beside her, and came at last to a clearing in the woods. Parked there was a little trailer painted deep green and scarlet, with tiny windows and a tin-pot chimney huffing smoke.

A man cleaning a harness was sitting on the steps of the trailer. Other men tended to a string of ponies that were tethered behind the camp. A woman in a long, crimson skirt with gold rings in her ears watched over a pot on a fire, from which good cooking smells drifted. Chantal, who had skipped lunch, felt her mouth water.

The boy broke free and ran to his mother, who picked him up and hugged him tightly. The gypsies stopped what they were doing and gathered around, pointing and exclaiming in their own language.

"He—was paddling in the river," Chantal stammered, backing off nervously. "The current can be tricky just there. He could have been in trouble. I thought I'd better bring him home."

"Wait!" said the man who had been on the steps. "One favor deserves another—it is the code of the Romany. We are the Loverage tribe. How can we show our gratitude, *gorgio* girl?"

Gorgio meant "nongypsy," Chantal knew. She swallowed hard.

There was only one thing that she craved, and that was to get back her nerve for riding. No one could give her that.

A shrill whinny made her look up. Tethered with the ponies was a pretty light gray mare with a full-flowing mane and tail. One glance, and Chantal was lost.

"You like the *grai*—the horse?" the gypsy man asked. "Jay will show you her paces."

A boy older than Chantal detached himself from the company and went to fetch the mare. Looping the simple rope reins over her neck, he vaulted nimbly onto her and cantered around, twisting the animal this way and that. Chantal watched them enviously. He made it look so easy. Horse and rider might almost have been one.

Bringing the mare to a halt beside her, Jay slipped down. "You try her now, lady?"

The old fear was rising, churning her stomach, turning her legs to rubber. "Well . . . maybe some other time," she hedged, longingly stroking the soft white muzzle. "What's her name?"

"She came to us in the mistral, so that's what we call her."

Mistral. It was the wind that swept the plains in the winter. Chantal thought of the wild horses that galloped before it with streaming manes and pluming tails, strong and free.

"You'll come again?" Jay asked.

"Maybe," Chantal replied.

She told no one about the episode, not even Mama. And something drew Chantal back to Mistral, even though she knew it was futile. Jay was there, grooming. "Here," he said, handing Chantal the brush. "Afterward, lead her around for exercise."

Mistral crunched up the mints that Chantal had brought and stood relaxed, waiting to be groomed. "Come on, girl," Chantal whispered. Untying the tether, she led the mare out of the woods to where the open plains beckoned. There the clouds rolled across the great wide bowl of the sky, driven by a wind that sent sweeping shadows across the landscape. It was wild and watery and very beautiful. Chantal wondered what it would be like to be on Mistral's back, cantering with the wind in her face and the ground rippling by, at ease and in control. That was the way she had been with Jonti before the bird had clapped up out of the grasses and spooked him.

Mistral nudged her shoulder as if to say, "Come on—ride me." Chantal gathered up the reins, but try as she might, she could not bring herself to climb on. Sad and dispirited, she led Mistral back to the string.

All week, the gypsies rolled in to set up camp in readiness for the festival. Some rumbled past the farm in oxcarts. Others arrived in battered old cars and vans or flashy horse trucks and modern trailers. None had the charm of the Loverage wagon, which Jay called a *vardo*.

"Where have you come from?" Chantal asked Jay.

"From the west," he replied. He drew himself up with pride. "This time I have been chosen to represent our tribe in the procession of Sara. It is a great honor. I will ride Mistral."

"I'll be there to watch you. We always go to the festival."

"Do you ride to the town?"

"Sometimes," Chantal said. Not this year, though. This time Papa was taking them in the car, and it was all because of her. Jay was studying her with that intense look that seemed to scrape the back of her skull. She had the feeling that he knew her terrible secret, that they all knew. Perhaps they were laughing at her. "The truth is, I'm afraid to ride," she blurted out. "My pony got spooked. I fell off and hurt myself."

"You should always get right back on, or otherwise the fear devil stakes his claim."

"I couldn't. By the time I was better, it was too late. It's a stupid fear! I wish I could overcome it!" Chantal cried passionately.

Jay was silent for a moment. Then he said, "Remember our promise? A Romany's word is sacred. You'll ride again one day, *gorgio* girl."

Festival day dawned fine. The Boiles set off early, but already the streets were thronged with people, all heading for the ancient church where the event took place. Gypsies were everywhere, some on foot with their children, some riding the sturdy white horses of the Camargue. Others drove them between the shafts and went rattling past with cries of "Watch your backs!" Chantal ranged through the crowd looking for the Loverages but did not see them.

"Let's stand here," said Mama, coming to a stop near the church. Andre went off to find his friends. Dad gave Chantal some money for candy.

"Don't get lost," Mama warned as she slipped away. She was cutting through a side street when Jay's father appeared. He looked desperate.

"Jay's been hurt and cannot take his place in the procession," he explained. "Mistral knows and trusts you. Jay says that you are the only one who can ride her. Will you do this for us?"

Chantal bit her lip. She couldn't let Jay down—or Mistral— who showed more faith in her, it seemed, than Chantal could give in return. The gypsy's glittering gaze was on her, willing her to accept. "Well, all right," she said nervously.

Mistral was prepared for the event, her coat gleaming, tack buffed to a fine finish, bit and stirrups shining. Jay, who seemed to be limping, held onto her head. "Hurry," he said to Chantal. "The other riders are waiting."

Steeling herself, Chantal scrambled onto Mistral's saddle. Once there, it felt astonishingly good to be on horseback again. "Walk on," she said.

Mistral moved forward with that lightness of step that made it seem as if her small hooves barely touched the ground. Feeling the salt-laden wind on her cheeks, smelling the sweetness of warm horseflesh as Mistral carried her along, Chantal wanted to shout for the sheer joy of it.

In the crowd her parents and Andre were growing anxious.

"Where can Chantal have gotten to?" Mama asked.

"She'll miss the show," Papa commented.

"Too late," said Andre. "Here they come!"

A hush fell upon the onlookers. Above the cries of seabirds and the distant churning of waves in the harbor came the magical drumbeat of many trampling hooves and the jingle of a silver harness. The lead rider appeared, sitting very upright in the saddle. His horse was excited, prancing sideways, nostrils flared and tail pluming. Following him came the gypsies from all over the world, riding proudly, sunlight gleaming off the muscled flanks of their mounts and twinkling on bits and shining leather. The statue of Sara that usually stood in the crypt was set in a carriage drawn by two Camargue horses. They would take her down to the shore and dip her in the tide to bless the waters and ensure good health and prosperity for the town.

People stamped and cheered. "Look!" Andre yelled in shocked surprise. "Mama, Papa. Look who's riding that white horse! It's Chantal!"

Papa aimed his camera. All three shouted and applauded. It was wonderful to see her on a horse again. Running alongside was a group of Romanies.

Chantal looked down from the saddle and saw Jay. "You're not hurt at all," she cried. "You tricked me!"

Jay grinned up at her, a saucy grin. "So? You're riding again, aren't you? Just like I said you would."

Chantal was quiet. Riding Mistral as a favor was all very well. The true test was getting up on Jonti again. She thought of her pony—eager, quick, nobody's fool. What if her nerve failed her?

Back home again, she wandered around the stable yard. She really had done it, she reasoned. She had ridden Mistral. Papa and Mama had talked about nothing else all the way home. Recalling the clatter of countless hooves and the way her heart had pounded in elation to the rhythm of Mistral's stride, Chantal had her answer. Of course she had not been afraid. There was nothing to be scared of.

She went straight to get Jonti. He butted her in rough affection, wanting a treat.

"Later," Chantal said. Swinging up onto his familiar gray back, she cantered off. A soft wind blew, lifting her hair. Far ahead, she saw a painted *vardo* trundling westward, followed by a string of horses. She squinted to see the white one near the end of the procession.

"Good-bye," she said, saluting. "And thank you." She had gotten her wish. She could ride again.

Driving Rosie

JENNY LAND

"Marie-Catherine!"

Marie heard her grandfather's voice before she saw him. Then he was there, kissing both of her cheeks. His tanned face glowed under his straw hat, and his strong arms wrapped around her. She could smell the familiar scent of horses on his clothes.

"Marie-Catherine! *Comment vas-tu?*"

Marie pulled away a bit. "Just Marie, Pépère. Everyone calls me Marie now." Eyeing her grandfather's puzzled expression, she added, "I'm fine, thank you. It's just that we don't speak French at home anymore; no one my age speaks it in Vermont."

"And what's wrong with speaking your mother tongue?" Pépère asked, tousling her chin-length hair. "Marie, then. That's fine. How is your sister?"

All of a sudden, the familiar, horrible knot came back to Marie's stomach. How could she have forgotten, even for a minute? "I don't know," she replied, staring at the ground. "Pretty sick, I guess."

Pépère frowned and then picked up Marie's bags and smiled. "She'll be better when your papa comes to get you next month. Your parents are just being careful, sending you to be with me while

Laurette is coming home from the hospital. They want to be sure that you don't catch polio too."

Marie smiled wanly. She couldn't help worrying that Laurette was even sicker than Mom and Dad were telling her. Her classmate Jimmy Reed had died of polio just a few weeks ago. What if she never saw Laurette again? Or, almost as terrible, what if Laurette never walked again? Marie wished she could be at home, to make sure that Laurette was all right.

Marie looked up at the sound of Pépère's whistle. He was striding toward the wagon and a new team of sleek brown horses. Their glossy tails twitched in the June sun. They looked alike, except one had a white blaze on the nose.

"Morgans, Marie! I traded in my old team. What do you think?"

I wish you'd traded them for a car! she thought, looking around at the station lot full of shiny cars. Pépère still wanted to drive horses? In 1952! She couldn't believe it.

Up on the wagon, Marie felt that everyone in Riverton was staring at her; she didn't see a single other horse in town. "Are there other horses anywhere, Pépère?"

Pépère laughed, startling the horses into a trot. "No, Marie, just farmers like me. I'd never trade them, though. I don't need to go anywhere, other than Riverton for supplies now and then, and I can't see loving a car like I do Jojo and Pierre. Can you? *Allez-y!*"

Pépère clicked his tongue to the horses. They pulled off onto a steep dirt road and started climbing up, past cornfields and wooden silos. Cars honked and whizzed around them. The horses breathed heavily; Marie could see sweat glistening on their backs.

From the top of the knoll, Marie could see rolling hills, Haybury down below, and the peaks of the White Mountains beyond. Despite all the jolting, she loved the feeling of the wind cutting through the heat of the day as they jostled down the steep open road and into Haybury.

Marie remembered the white church on the corner, the green store with the benches out front, the row of houses along Main Street. Pépère rounded the bend, and there they were, right at the yellow house and barn, just as she remembered them.

Pépère pulled Marie's bags off the wagon. "You run inside, Marie. Remember where your room is, right? I've got something quick to tend to in the barn, and then we'll have a meal before milking time."

Marie took her bags and went inside. The house smelled faded, musty, just as it always had. She went right up the central stairway, into the eaves. Her room was on the right in her grandmother's old sewing room. Mémère had died before she was born, but Marie always felt close to her in this low room with its bright crocheted afghans and its colored glass ornaments in the window. She set her bags on the narrow bed. She and Laurette usually shared this bed. It seemed strange to have so much room to herself.

"Marie-Catherine? *À la soupe!*" Pépère called up the stairs.

Marie hurried downstairs and sat down at the kitchen table, where Pépère was already ladling orange soup into bowls. Carrot soup. She felt embarrassingly ill.

"Pépère?"

"Yes, *bijou?*"

"I—I'm sorry." Marie spoke fast; she knew that Pépère had made the meal just for her. "Carrots make me feel sick. I'm really sorry."

Pépère laughed. "No problem there; we can have sandwiches. Too hot for soup, anyhow. I wasn't expecting it, judging from what I heard on the radio this morning."

Had it really only been this morning that she had last been at home? Marie's gaze blurred; she remembered her last peek at Laurette, lying hot and restless, lost in a sea of pillows on their parents' bed. She'd been asleep, so Marie had only whispered good-bye.

Pépère's chuckle startled her back to the kitchen table. "You're just like Rosie!"

"Who's Rosie?" Marie asked.

"Rosie's the old chestnut mare I got from Mrs. Lewis this winter, not long before I bought Jojo and Pierre. You remember Mrs. Lewis, over in Haybury Center? She babysat you once. Well, anyhow, she finally got too old to take care of herself, let alone the horse, so she asked me if I'd take Rosie. That horse still has a lot of spunk. Never heard of a horse that hated carrots before, but she's one, for sure. The two of you and carrots," Pépère laughed.

"I didn't say I hated carrots, Pépère." Marie's cheeks burned red. "I just got sick from them last year."

"Well, maybe that explains what happened to Rosie. Finish your milk, and I'll take you out to meet her. I'll bet you haven't seen a horse since last summer. Have any of your friends got one?"

Marie swallowed her milk and shook her head. Hardly, in the

middle of Montpelier, she thought. She tried to imagine a horse in her neighborhood, among the rows of houses, and failed. True, her own house had a nice big yard, across from the sawmill where Dad worked, but she still didn't know a single kid with a horse. Quietly, Marie followed Pépère outside and over to the barn. She wished Laurette was here to hunt for the barn kittens or play in the hayloft.

"*Ne t'inquiète pas*, Marie-Catherine," Pépère told her, reading her thoughts. "Don't worry. Laurette will be here soon enough."

Marie took a deep breath, watching the familiar row of black-and-white Holsteins survey her. She followed Pépère into a smaller attached barn, past Jojo's and Pierre's stalls, and then over to a further stall that she hadn't noticed before. She walked down and peered in.

BAM! A huge head swung from the side and banged into Marie's own head, almost knocking her over.

"Rosie!" Pépère scolded. "We've got company. This is Marie." Then he added to Marie, "Don't worry, you just startled her. And you should do fine together—she only speaks English too."

Pépère winked at Marie and pulled several leather straps off the stable wall. He went into the stall, soothing Rosie, and harnessed her up. The horse turned her head sideways again in order to survey Marie. Her flaxen mane stood straight up, refusing to lie flat, and her eyes looked wicked, daring.

"Are you sure she's all right to ride, Pépère?" Marie asked uncertainly.

Pépère smiled. "Oh, you won't ride this one," he replied, stroking Rosie's smooth nose. "She's too old and bowlegged for that; she's really a pony for pulling a cart. That's what she's trained to do. Come on, the trap's out back. It's high time you learned to drive, Marie, with all your time on this farm; I don't know how you got out of it last year."

Pépère guided Rosie out through the stall door, out of the

barn. Rosie stood patiently as Pépère hitched her up to the old trap with wide wooden wheels.

"She'll be your friend forever if you take her for a ride," Pépère told Marie. "Climb on up there. Now, take the reins and bring them down gently on her haunches and pull them back to stop. Give that a try."

Marie climbed onto the driver's seat, resting her feet on the bar in front, and stared at Rosie's back. Rosie stood alert, ears pricked up. Marie took the reins uncertainly.

"Go on, tap her," Pépère said. "Giddyap outta that there then, you Rosie!"

As soon as Marie brought down the reins, she and Rosie went flying down the barn path toward the pasture.

"WHOA!" Pépère yelled. "I said tap her, Marie!"

But Rosie kept galloping onward, and Marie jolted behind her, along the fence, and into the uncut hay field. There, Rosie abruptly stopped and began munching on the tall timothy grass.

Marie laughed. "I know what she likes to eat now!" she yelled over her shoulder at Pépère, who was hurrying toward them along the lane. She left the reins on the seat and went to Rosie's side. She stroked her knobby shoulder. "We'll get along, old girl," Marie whispered to her. "No carrots, I promise."

From then on, the days passed quickly. Marie got up at seven, just as Pépère was coming in for a second breakfast after finishing the milking. Marie helped with the dishes and then went outside to get Rosie. Almost before Marie knew it, one week had passed— and then another.

Rosie looked forward to Marie's visits. At first, Marie led her with a rope around the stable yard. Marie learned to let Rosie know that she was walking into the stall with a gentle clicking sound so that Rosie would move to the right side for harnessing. Rosie gradually agreed to take the bit from her, and Marie stood on a box to reach up and fasten the bridle behind Rosie's ears.

Then Marie put on the halter and breeching strap and led Rosie outside to hitch up. She guided Rosie with a gentle pull on the reins, without pulling too hard on one side so that the trap didn't go around in circles. Rosie, for her part, seemed to understand Marie's voice. Within a few weeks, Marie took Rosie all the way down Main Street to the store. She hitched up Rosie outside and ran in to buy a cheery postcard of a field of red clover for Laurette.

Marie couldn't wait to hear news from home. Finally, one afternoon Marie and Pépère drove Rosie over to the post office in Haybury Center. Mrs. Lewis' neighbors came down from their porches to wave.

"Hey, Mr. Chevalier!" called one man. "Pretty fine horsewoman there to escort you to town. Is that Rosie there?"

Marie waved back. Rosie sure looked happier than she had for a long while; she looked sleek, perky, and almost young. Her mane stuck up higher than ever. She almost leaped out of the stall whenever she saw Marie come in with her halter; she loved to pull the trap. Marie wondered if Rosie had been depressed for the past few months, without a job to do.

At the post office a large, pleasant woman ushered them back behind the counter.

Pépère picked up the phone and cleared his throat. "Ah, yes, Mrs. Walters. This is George. I'm trying to reach the Chevalier family on Water Street in Montpelier. . . . Yes. C-H-E-V-A-L-I-E-R. Like a horseman." He winked at Marie, and she blinked back, surprised. She'd never thought of what her last name meant before.

"*Allo? Oui?* Marguerite? It's Papa here. Yes . . . yes. Marie's here. She's fine. I know, it's long distance. How is Laurette?"

Marie counted the floorboards, almost too afraid to listen.

"She's still getting better?" Pépère paused again and then nodded gravely. "Don't worry, I'll tell her . . . yes. We'll see you in a few weeks. *Oui. Au revoir.*" Pépère slowly hung up the phone and let out a long, slow breath.

Marie forced herself to stop counting floorboards. "How is she?"

Pépère looked down at Marie and smiled. He put his arm around her. "She's getting better, Marie. She'll come with your parents next month."

They walked back out to the desk, and Pépère gave the lady some change. Outside, Pépère patted Marie on the shoulder. "I'll drive us home."

What's wrong? Marie wondered. Something had to be wrong. They started down the street, Rosie jogging steadily along.

"What else did Mom have to say?" Marie finally asked.

Pépère looked at her sadly. "Laurette won't walk properly again, Marie." He paused and slowed Rosie to a walk but soon absently slacked the reins so that she began to trot again. "That happens to some kids with polio. But she's getting better, much better, and she wants to see you."

Marie stared at the roadside grass. Not walk? Laurette, her tomboy little sister? No hide-and-seek . . . no races on the way to school . . .

"Will she be in a wheelchair, Pépère?"

"*Oui, bijou.* She probably will. Or at least in braces."

Marie remained quiet for the rest of the way home. She took Rosie inside her stall as Pépère went off to do the milking. After drying off the harness, Marie combed down Rosie and gave her a lump of sugar.

"What will we do, Rosie?" Marie asked the chestnut horse. "Laurette loves playing outside. It's not fair."

Rosie snacked thoughtfully, her limpid eyes gazing at Marie.

"How would you help her, Rosie?" Marie continued aimlessly, smoothing Rosie's unruly mane. Rosie neighed.

Marie looked up suddenly. She had a plan. "Of course!" She threw an arm around Rosie, latched the stall door, and ran into the cow barn. "Pépère!"

"*Qu'est-ce qu'il y a?* What is it, Marie-Catherine?" Pépère replied anxiously, appearing from behind one of the huge Holstein cows.

"No, everything's fine, Pépère; it's just that I've thought of something! Laurette can drive Rosie! She loves animals! You know how she's always asking Mom and Dad if we can have another dog or keep chickens out back."

Pépère looked puzzled. "You mean take Rosie?"

"And the neighborhood kids will be excited to see Rosie; it'll be so much better than a wheelchair!"

Pépère's face uncreased, and he started to laugh. "*Bien sûr,* Marie-Catherine! A horse gives the best transportation! If this horse could talk, you bet she'd say that she'd go with you! But where will Rosie stay?"

"There's that shed on the side of the house where Dad keeps the Ford in the winter . . . I think it's an old barn. It's perfect, Pépère!"

Pépère swung Marie around. "You and Rosie will make Laurette such a happy girl!" he exclaimed.

Marie spent the next few days getting the house ready for Laurette, bringing in bouquets of buttercups and clover from the field. She made a special bouquet with roses from the front yard to make Mémère's sewing room smell nice. She made a batch of maple cookies, Laurette's favorite, and hid them in the pantry so that Pépère wouldn't eat them.

"She'll love you," Marie assured Rosie the final evening in the barn, bringing her a large handful of timothy grass. "So be good to her."

Rosie twitched her tail agreeably.

The next day the morning dragged. When noon finally arrived, Marie sat on the fence out front. Two teams of workhorses passed by—then silence.

Finally, she heard a rumble in the distance. "The Ford!" she yelled, jumping up. "Pépère, they're here!"

Sure enough, the blue Ford came around the bend from the store and rolled into the driveway. Dad climbed out right away. "Marie!" he called. And Mom was heading back to the trunk, pulling out some metal braces. Marie ran over to the window and looked in. Laurette looked thin and tired.

"Hi, Marie." Laurette spoke fast, sounding anxious. She reached up to Dad, holding his waist. "Marie, you know—" she paused as she pulled out some crutches, "—I can't walk anymore. Not like I used to, anyway."

Marie felt sad as she looked at Laurette, but she smiled bravely. "But you're already so much better. And we've got a surprise for you! Pépère!"

Around from the side of the barn came Pépère in the trap. "*Bonjour, mes petites!* This is Rosie, a new friend for Laurette."

Marie looked at Laurette—she looked confused. "Laurette, you can drive her! I'll teach you how! She's wonderful! Pépère's going to give her to you, and she can live at home on Water Street in the shed." Marie looked nervously at Mom and Dad, but they

were already grinning. "Pépère! You called them yesterday and told them!"

"*Oui,*" Pépère admitted sheepishly. "I had to be sure before you told Laurette. But it was all Marie's idea, Laurette. And I think you should go for a drive together." He got down out of the trap and picked up Laurette, helping her up next to Marie. "Show her how, Marie."

Marie looked at her sister, and Laurette smiled back. "You tap her gently with the reins," Marie told Laurette, handing them to her. Then she looked back over her shoulder. *"Au revoir,* Pépère! *Merci encore!"*

Off they went, flashing out of the driveway. Behind them, Mom called out anxiously, but Marie saw Pépère cup his hands to his mouth.

"You're the Chevalier sisters, for sure!" he called.

Laughing, Marie held her sister's hand together with the reins, and on they went down the road, into the noon sunshine.

Joey's Last Gallop

CINDY JEFFERIES

Emily and Jessica stared at the image of a great white horse, high up on the hillside. It looked as if a giant child had taken some chalk and drawn the horse on an enormous piece of green, hillside paper.

"Who made it?" Emily asked. She was on a visit from America with her mom.

"Nobody knows," her mom said. "But it's thousands of years old, and lots of people must have worked together, digging the turf away from the white stone underneath."

When they got home, Jessica and Emily went down to the pasture to see Joey, the white pony. Their moms, Sue and Allie, were sisters, and Joey had been their pony when they were little. Now he was very old and wasn't ridden anymore.

"You've got two white horses," Emily teased Jessica. "But you can't ride either of them!"

Jessica didn't mind. Although she would have liked a pony to ride, like Emily had in America, she'd known Joey all her life. She had the great white horse on the hill to admire and old Joey to love, and that was good enough for her.

Joey's white coat had grown long and shaggy. He spent many hours standing under the old apple tree, dreaming perhaps of days long ago, when he had won ribbons for Sue and Allie at the local show. Now they were grown up and had girls of their own, and it was Jessica who brought him an apple in her pocket.

Joey's blanket had slipped, so Jessica tugged it straight for him, while Emily broke the ice in his water bucket. There was plenty of straw in his shed, but Joey only went inside when it was wet and stormy. On a night like this, when the grass was sparkling with frost like the stars in the dark sky, he preferred to be out, under the tree.

"Come on. Let's go in. I'm freezing!" Jessica gave Joey a last pat and followed Emily inside.

"I don't know how he can stand it, being outside on a night like this!" Emily told her mom when the girls were back in the kitchen.

"Oh, honey, Joey's always been an outdoor pony," her mom said with a smile. "He's not used to the warm California climate, like you are!"

"Do you remember when we were girls and tried to shut him in one cold night?" Sue reminded Allie. "He almost kicked the door down until he was let out again!"

Much later, after the girls had gone to sleep, something woke Jessica. She got out of bed and tiptoed to the window. The full moon shone on the narrow road, making it look like a hard, black river. There wasn't a breath of wind. What had disturbed her on such a quiet night? She looked over toward Joey's pasture and gasped.

"Joey!"

Jessica was sure that she and Emily had closed the gate, but Joey was out, making his way slowly toward the house. What was he doing? She ought to get her mom. A car might come along. There could be an accident!

Emily was sleeping, so Jessica pulled on her bathrobe and shoved her feet into her slippers.

"Mom!" But Sue was deeply asleep, and Allie was too. Jessica couldn't bear to wake them. Instead she pulled her bathrobe close and crept downstairs. Someone had to take Joey back to his pasture.

She took a carrot from the vegetable basket and unlocked the back door. It was freezing outside. Her slippers left a clear trail through the crunchy, frozen grass.

"Come on Joey," she said, patting his neck. "What are you doing here? You should be in your pasture. And what have you done with your blanket? I'm sure I fastened it tightly."

The old pony stood quietly at the side of the road. He looked at Jessica and nuzzled her shoulder. He was pleased to see her, but there was no way that she could get him to move. No matter how much she tried to turn his head for home, it was no use. Joey planted his feet stubbornly in the frozen grass and refused to budge. He wasn't even tempted by the carrot.

At last Jessica got so cold that she climbed up onto his back and hugged him for warmth.

"What am I going to do with you?" she scolded. "You can't stay here all night!" She broke the carrot into pieces and leaned down to give him some. She couldn't be angry with him for long.

She had decided to go back inside and get her mom after all, when Joey's ears pricked up. He lifted his head and looked down the road. At first Jessica could hear nothing, but then Joey whinnied, and Jessica heard an answering neigh. Soon she could hear hooves on the road. Who would be out riding at this time of night?

"Maybe it's Mrs. Thompson on Strider," she told Joey hopefully. "She goes out at all kinds of funny times. She'll help me get you back. You'll follow Strider, won't you?"

But it wasn't Mrs. Thompson on Strider. It was the gray hunter, Shadow, who lived on the farm nearby. Shadow was walking up the middle of the road all by herself, and when she drew level with Jessica and Joey, she stopped.

"How did you get out?" asked Jessica in amazement. The hunter took no notice of her but touched noses with Joey before snorting noisily.

A few moments later two dapple-grays that Jessica had never seen before trotted up. Then a huge racehorse from the stables in Lambourn arrived. Jessica recognized him because he'd been in the newspaper recently, famous for winning almost every race there was. His name was White Chocolate, and his creamy mane felt like silk when Jessica leaned over to stroke him. He, too, touched noses with Joey and then stood quietly beside the old pony.

Jessica couldn't think of what to do. What was going on? How had all these horses and ponies gotten out? And why were they all coming here?

"Go home!" she said to White Chocolate. She tried to slap his rump to send him back down the road, but he only turned toward her and breathed warm, stable smells at her. Jessica could no more send these horses home than turn back an incoming tide.

Soon the whole road was filled with horses and ponies, and every single one was white. They came from all directions, from up the road and down, from the woods and through the fields, all to touch noses with Joey. Then, although no one gave a signal that Jessica could hear, the whole herd set off up the road together.

"No, Joey, not you!" Jessica wailed as Joey took his place in front, next to White Chocolate. But it was too late for Jessica to dismount and go for help. The pace was picking up, and still more white horses were arriving, cantering up to greet Joey before dropping back to take their places in the strange, moonlit procession. They trotted up the road to where a path led to the great white horse carved into the hill.

Joey was sometimes a little unsteady on his feet, but now his gait was strong and assured. He seemed to be growing younger by the minute. Once on the path he started to canter, and Jessica held on tight to his mane. As the canter became a gallop, one of Jessica's slippers was lost, and she flung her arms around his neck to hang on.

At the end of the path was the hill, and the horses spread out over the grass. While Joey had been galloping, even more horses and ponies had arrived, and now hundreds of hooves were thundering up the hill in the pale light. Joey galloped right up to the top, never even pausing for breath.

At the top he stopped, and the others halted with him. The only sound in the crisp night was of hundreds of horses breathing, and the air around them was wreathed in mist from their steaming bodies. Jessica looked for the familiar patches of bare chalk that made the great white horse, but to her astonishment, they were gone! This hill was as green as the rest of the hills that surrounded her house.

Then a stir of excitement ran through the horses. Their ranks were parting, leaving a clear path. Joey started to walk along it, and Jessica strained to see what they were approaching. Was it steam from the horses, or was there really something there?

The shape flickered and trembled, a leg here, a wisp of tail there, churning and turning in the mist. Closer and closer Joey took Jessica, while she shrank down on his back. It was a colossal horse. She could see that he was not a tame animal. His huge, stony hooves were unshod, his mane untrimmed, and his flinty eyes were as wild as a November night.

Jessica was as frightened as she had ever been in her life. She wanted to believe that she was in a dream, but her one bare foot was icy cold, and she knew that she was wide-awake.

Calmly, quietly, old Joey walked on until the great white horse was towering over both of them. Jessica squeezed her eyes shut. She buried her face in Joey's mane. She couldn't bear to look.

But then she could hear the great white horse and Joey whinny to each other, like Joey did to Jessica when she took him his evening treat of apples or sugar. For a moment, Jessica felt the cold breath of the great white horse upon her, and then it was gone.

Joey turned and started to gallop. Around and around the hill, all of the horses wheeled together, plowing up the frozen ground with their hooves. Jessica's hair and her bathrobe were streaming out behind her. To one side of Joey, White Chocolate raced; on the other, Shadow kept up. The dapple-grays followed behind.

Jessica gripped with her knees, sat up, and laughed with excitement at the wild gallop. She and old Joey were having the time of their lives!

All too soon, Joey turned for the path, and the other horses followed. Jessica looked back for the great white horse, but he

was gone.

Now the horses' sides were heaving, and Joey's back felt damp with sweat. Jessica stroked his thick neck fondly.

"We have to find that blanket," she told him. "You can't catch a chill."

The herd was breaking up, with horses and ponies disappearing in all directions. By the time they had reached home, only Shadow was left. She and Joey blew gently at each other before she trotted back to her farm.

Jessica rode Joey gently along the road until they reached his pasture. She soon spotted his blanket, lying forgotten on the grass, and slipped off his back to get it. He followed her happily enough as she took him into his shed to rub him down. After she'd fastened the blanket carefully, she leaned her head against his shoulder and gave him a hug.

"Oh, Joey," she said. "I'll never forget tonight!" She felt in her bathrobe pocket and found the rest of the carrot, which he munched on contentedly. After she'd made sure that his gate was secure, she ran across the icy grass and went back to bed.

Jessica slept late, but eventually the winter sun that was shining through the curtains woke her. She could only find one slipper, but she threw on her bathrobe and ran downstairs. Sue, Allie, and Emily were sitting quietly in the kitchen with cups of tea. To her surprise, Jessica realized that her mom had been crying.

"It's Joey," Mom said. "He died last night."

In the shed Joey was lying on the straw, looking as if he was asleep.

"He must have been feeling sick and came in here to lie down," said Mom. "Then his heart stopped. He didn't suffer. He died in his sleep."

Jessica thought that she might cry. Then she remembered last night. He'd been ready. He'd come to say good-bye. And how he'd enjoyed his last, wild gallop!

Jessica put her arms around her mom and gave her a hug. "Don't be sad, Mom," she said. "Joey's happy."

And somehow, she knew that it was true.

Red

JENNY OLDFIELD

I call him "Red" for short.

His long name is "Pride of the Red Desert," grandson of top Australian show jumper Ayers Rock. His mother is the world-famous Ocean's Pride. What an amazing, beautiful horse. *My* horse!

Red stands 16.2 hands high. His chestnut coat gleams somewhere between copper and flame; his mane has colors in it that don't even have names.

I've known him since I was ten and he was five years old, when Dad took a chance and bought him from a training yard in the south. We brought him up north. The first owner said Red was "disappointing," but boy, was he wrong. Red and I proved that in a hundred competitions. We're proving it now, in the run-up to the Olympics.

The thing about Red is that he only works for me. Stick another rider on his back, and he doesn't want to know. Red-and-Abbi. Abbi-and-Red. You can't separate us.

So we're driving to the Northern Eventing Trials. We come off the highway and park in the grounds of a big country estate with a hundred other top-of-the-line, state-of-the-art trailers.

Before I even say "hi" to anyone, I check that Red's journey has been okay.

"Hey," I say, running my hand down his strong back and then over his legs. I take off the travel boots and tail bandage. "We're here safe and sound. This is a big event for us, Red. If we get placed here, we're practically on our way to the Olympics!"

Red lowers his head and nuzzles me on my shoulder. *Take it easy. No problem,* he seems to say.

"Abbi, stop gossiping with the horse and bring him out to grass," Dad yells and then scoots off to find our stable.

Red sighs and stamps on the floor of the trailer. *Let me out. Show me what there is to eat.*

"Hi!" I say to Will Redknapp, who's in the trailer next to me with his gray mare, Himalayan Snow. And "hi" to Jack Moreton, with another chestnut gelding, All About Me, on the other side.

Red strides down the ramp like he's the king. And he is.

"Number fifteen." Dad dashes back, eager to get Red settled with a nice bed of shavings, clean water, and a bucket of feed. We've got his diet, exercise, and sleep figured out to the last detail. Red is an athlete—1,200 pounds of gleaming muscle and sinew.

Dad vanishes again to talk to the event organizers, and I take care of Red—brushing and polishing, combing and braiding. It's stuff that I can do blindfolded—I've done it so often.

Red is happy. He likes me fussing over him. He glides into his stable, turns, and looks out over his door like he's ready to begin. *Where are the judges? Let's go!*

"Nervous?" Dad asks me that night over supper.

We're in a big tent with all of the other riders and trainers. There are long tables loaded with food. Everyone's talking horses, horses, horses.

I nod.

"Good!" he grins. "The weather forecast says fine with a few light showers. Not too hot."

I take a deep breath and imagine riding Red out into the arena.

"We're here. We've done all we can." Dad reminds me of the work that we've put in over the last year, how we've brought Red to his peak at exactly the right time. "Now go out there and enjoy it, Abbi. Whatever happens, I'll be more proud of you than I can say."

I grin back. I want to win. I want to be on the Olympic team. I don't say it, but we both know it.

The sun shines through light clouds, and there's a good crowd for day one, dressage. An hour before my slot I ride Red into the practice area, set back from the main arena.

"More right leg, keep your hands absolutely still, that's it, now a touch with your left leg!" Dad yells.

Red responds to the slightest shift of my weight. His transition on the diagonal from trot to canter is as smooth as silk.

After 20 minutes Dad is happy and tells me to go and get changed.

That means my tailored black coat, sleek white jodhpurs, black boots up to my knees, and a hat that looks like a top hat that someone sat on and squashed. It sounds weird, but when I glance in the mirror, I can't help feeling excited.

When I get back, Red is gleaming, braided perfection.

"Next to ride is our youngest competitor, Abigail Edwards, on Pride of the Red Desert," the guy announces over the loudspeaker.

Dad goes to sit in the trainers' stand. Now it's just me and my horse. Dressage is all about accuracy. You count the steps; you aim for markers. Total concentration. One foot wrong, and you lose points.

It's not Red's favorite event, but he does it perfectly for me—the lead changes and the extended trot, neck arched, chin tucked in, high stepping across the green turf.

"Good boy!" I murmur as I bow to the judges at the end of the test. We've zigzagged and circled, turned and twisted. The crowd claps for us. We pass Will Redknapp on Himalayan Snow. They're next.

"Good job!" Will grins at me. No nasty, sneery stuff from him, not like you sometimes get from Jack Moreton. I wish Will luck.

The scoring's complicated. You aim to chalk up as few penalty points as you can. At the end of the day I come out tied for second place with Will Redknapp and another rider named Alice McPhee. We are behind Jack Moreton on All About Me.

Day two is show jumping—big hurdles, walls, and hedges set up inside the arena. This is more Red's thing. He has the longest legs, the strongest hindquarters.

"Remember, Abbi, don't force him to take that last corner too tight." Dad's worried that I'll push Red too hard. "You need five full strides before the triple."

"We can do it in four," I argue. "It's going to be a matter of split-second timing, and with the mood Red is in, I think it's worth taking a few risks."

Dad looks doubtful but leaves it to Red and me.

It seems like a long wait before we get into the arena. Enough time to see that most of the horses make mistakes at the big brick wall—that and the water jump.

Alice gets penalty points for a refusal. Will and Jack both make it clear.

"Beat that!" Jack says to me as he rides out of the arena.

"Next to go is Pride of the Red Desert with Abigail Edwards." I'm frowning with concentration, and Dad lets go of Red's reins.

Red prances a few steps into the arena, so proud, so full of energy.

We're surrounded by painted red-and-white rails, fake bushes, and walls. I wait for the bell, and then we take off. I rise in the stirrups over the first fence. We're flying, Red and me.

Over the water, clear so far. But should I risk the sharp turn and four strides before the last triple? The time's tight. Yeah, four strides. Red feels me turn him hard and knows that I'm asking a lot of him.

Okay, gotcha! he tells me.

He turns fast and takes the triple like a rocket. A back hoof clips the rail. I turn and watch it. The rail shudders but stays put, and we cross the finish line.

Red is all sweaty. I'm out of breath.

"That's fantastic work from Abigail Edwards and Pride of the Red Desert!" the announcer tells the crowd.

There are cheers ringing in my ears and tears in my eyes as I walk Red out into the practice arena. I jump down and put my arms around his neck.

Hey, he seems to say. *Why the waterworks? Didn't we just move up to tie for first?*

My horse is so laid-back that he's practically falling over!

"I love you!" I tell him. "And it's not just because you can jump higher, faster, farther than any other horse. It's because of who you are."

He understands every word I say.

Dad and I sleep in the bunks in the front of the trailer. They're snug and smell like Red.

Only I can't sleep. I'm looking out the window at the starry sky, worrying about tomorrow. Day three and the cross-country. At one o'clock. I pull on my jeans and boots and, without waking Dad, sneak out to the stables.

Red is curled up on a mound of wood shavings, his legs tucked under him, looking ungainly, as horses do when they're lying down.

But he raises his head and snickers at me and then lets me settle down next to him, leaning against his shoulder. This is us off duty—me in my jeans and sweatshirt, Red with his mane hanging loose, with specks of wood shavings caught up in it.

I pick them out one by one, thinking about the six years that I've owned him—getting to know each other, deciding that we could get along after I'd learned what to do and what not to do. Red has a sensitive mouth and hates it when you pull the bit around—I got thrown off a couple of times. I only use the lightest tack now. It took us a few years to make a real team.

Then the hard work. Up every morning at six, working in the indoor arena. And every evening, taking him over jumps. Then weekends, traveling all over the country, winning trophies, and slowly improving until we got on the list of Olympic hopefuls, right at the top of our sport.

"We're going to make it!" I whisper to my Pride of the Red Desert.

His deep, even breathing tells me that he's asleep.

I'm up at dawn, mucking out the stable, snatching a quick breakfast with Dad before we walk the three-and-a-half-mile course together. It's a tough one. We have to figure out the best angles over pine trunks piled six feet high, across rough grassland, through woods to the birch fence, then the trailer jump, then a high stone wall—the real thing, not fake. You name anything you might come across in the countryside, and somewhere there's a cross-country fence built like it.

We're high on a ridge by this time, and the wind is up. Dad and I pace out the distance between fences. I'm thinking, *This is definitely a challenge.*

Dad doesn't say much until we're back at the stable, grooming and tacking up.

"You know what you're doing?

I nod. "It's all in my head."

"We're in a great position. Tied for first."

I nod again. The knot in my stomach gets worse, so I grab a currycomb and give Red's coat one last flick.

"We're not under any pressure," Dad goes on. "Everyone's

expecting Jack Moreton and Will Redknapp to do well—they're the more experienced ones."

"We'll hang in there," I promise him. My stomach's grinding away like a cement mixer. I try not to let it show.

Dad takes the currycomb from me. "Go and get changed, Abbi. I'll finish tacking up."

Those fences are huge! I think as I put on my helmet.

I catch a glimpse of the finish line as I cross back to the stables. A riderless horse canters home, reins and stirrups flapping. I see one of the stewards catch him and think that everything's okay.

"Ready!" Dad says, giving me a leg up, eager to lead us out. I'm in the saddle, walking out to the start, feeling thousands of expectant eyes looking at us.

"Hey, Abbi!" A woman steps forward. "Can I get a photo with you and Red?"

Dad and I don't have time to object before this fan is grabbing Red's reins way too hard and smiling toward a camera held by another woman.

Click, click—the photo gets taken, the fan lets go, and we walk on.

Red strides with total calm, until a stray scrap of litter spooks the riderless horse.

He goes up on his hind legs and crashes down, just inches away from Red. This spooks Red, too, and he tugs the reins out of Dad's hands, to the crowd's shock.

I steady Red, and Dad catches up.

"Okay?" he checks.

"Yeah, no problem."

The announcement comes up over the speakers. It's our turn.

"Go for it!" Dad whispers.

I'm finding my balance as Red surges forward across the rough grass, the course spread out before us.

We're galloping downhill to the first jump, the pyramid of pine trunks. I can almost smell the resin. There's a blur of spectators' faces on both sides of the white tape, and Red's hooves thud on the soft ground.

Then it happens.

Without warning, as I put pressure on the right rein to steer my horse to the edge of the jump, the bridle breaks. Maybe because of the near miss with the gray or the spectator hanging onto the bridle so tightly, the leather strap connecting the rein to the metal ring snaps. The bit slides out of Red's mouth and trails close to the ground.

I hear a groan from the crowd. My heart plummets. That's it. The end. Good-bye to the Olympic Games. Good-bye, our dream.

We're two strides away from the trunks. I feel Red falter as the rein trails loose for a fraction of a second. Then he picks up speed again. He surges on.

I have no control. Red looks at the jump and decides to go ahead. He tilts his weight back on his haunches and then launches himself. We're flying. I let go of the useless reins and grab a handful of mane. We're over the trunks, landing, racing on.

"Go, Red!" I urge, leaning close to his ear.

All of that gleaming muscle is working, pounding over the ground, at a flat-out gallop toward the second fence.

Can we do this? I ask myself. *Can I stay in the saddle?*

Red has no doubts. The second jump takes us uphill to the coffin—there's a deep trench dug on the far side of a tall brushwood fence. A horse can lose its footing and crash down into the dark hole, rider and all.

"Go!" I whisper.

He's strong and sure. I use my legs against his flanks to guide him. We're over and clear, galloping on.

By now word has gotten around. *Pride of the Red Desert has lost his bridle. Abbi Edwards is sticking with it, but she'll never complete the*

course like that! I see an ambulance cruising toward us at the far side of the woods.

They're guessing without Red. I'm glued to his back, and he wants to compete. He races on, through the trees, soaring over the birch fence and onward.

My amazing, beautiful horse. What can I say?

We clatter across the trailer jump and then over a stream; we gallop through the countryside, sail over hedges, rush toward the finish line.

"Go, Red!" I cry. I have a fistful of mane and a huge wave of hope in my heart.

The crowd is cheering. *She did it! She rode him without a bridle!* I see my dad waiting for us at the end of the course.

We arrive. The shouts deafen me.

The air rasps in my dry throat; my heart pounds as I slide from the saddle. I'm hugging Red. Dad is hugging me.

They take photographs; the organizers push back the crowd.

Red holds up his head. His sides heave, and his neck is dark with sweat. I'm crying into his mane, and I'm holding him tight in the photo that appears in the papers the next day.

WONDER HORSE! it says in big headlines, after the selectors choose us for the Olympic team. ABBI-AND-RED HEAD FOR GOLD!

Acknowledgments

The publisher would like to thank the copyright holders for permission to reproduce the following copyright material:

Rosemary Chiba: "Inkblack" text copyright © Rosemary Chiba 2005; **Gill Harvey:** "The Rivals" text copyright © Gill Harvey 2005; **Elizabeth Holland:** "A Horse Without Equal" text copyright © Elizabeth Holland 2005; **Cindy Jefferies:** "Joey's Last Gallop" text copyright © Cindy Jefferies 2005; **Pamela Kavanagh:** "Ride Like the Wind" text copyright © Pamela Kavanagh 2005; **Jenny Land:** "Driving Rosie" text copyright © Jenny Land 2005; **Jenny Oldfield:** "The Last Roundup" and "Red" text copyright © Jenny Oldfield 2005; **Judy Paterson:** "The Parking Lot Pony" text copyright © Judy Paterson 2005; **Rebecca Kraft Rector:** "Little Miss Perfect and Me" text copyright © Rebecca Kraft Rector 2005; **Lois Ruby:** "Madrigal's Melody" text copyright © Lois Ruby 2005; **Matilda Webb:** "A Different Kind of Pony" text copyright © Matilda Webb 2005

The publishers would like to thank the artists for their illustrations as follows:

Bruce Emmett: illustrations for "The Last Roundup" and "Ride Like the Wind" copyright © Bruce Emmett 2005; **Layne Johnson:** illustrations for "A Different Kind of Pony," "Driving Rosie," and "Red" copyright © Layne Johnson 2005; **Richard Jones:** illustrations for "Little Miss Perfect and Me" and "The Rivals" copyright © Richard Jones 2005; **Angelo Rinaldi:** illustrations for "Joey's Last Gallop," "Madrigal's Melody," and "The Parking Lot Pony" copyright © Angelo Rinaldi 2005; **Sally Taylor:** illustrations for "A Horse Without Equal" and "Inkblack" copyright © Sally Taylor 2005